*Joe, trapped with the ball when a defender broke through on Coley and made a pitchout impossible, turned and looked toward a run inside. That avenue was blocked. So he turned farther, knowing without a moment's doubt that Tracy, seeing Joe's dilemma, would somehow get himself free for a pass. And sure enough, there was Tracy, loping into the open. Joe fired the ball across the field and Tracy caught it. A loss of yardage turned into a gain becuase Joe knew where Tracy would be, and Tracy knew Joe would be looking for him.*

*How many times, Joe wondered, had he been saved by his friends in the backfield?*

"Dygard scores again. . . . Readers will enjoy the gridiron action and easily relate to Joe's dilemma."
—*Booklist*

"*Backfield Package* is a fine read."
—*School Library Journal*

# BACKFIELD PACKAGE

## Thomas J. Dygard

PUFFIN BOOKS

PUFFIN BOOKS
Published by the Penguin Group
Penguin Books USA Inc., 375 Hudson Street, New York, New York 10014, U.S.A.
Penguin Books Ltd, 27 Wrights Lane, London W8 5TZ, England
Penguin Books Australia Ltd, Ringwood, Victoria, Australia
Penguin Books Canada Ltd, 10 Alcorn Avenue, Toronto, Ontario, Canada M4V 3B2
Penguin Books (N.Z.) Ltd, 182–190 Wairau Road, Auckland 10, New Zealand

Penguin Books Ltd, Registered Offices: Harmondsworth, Middlesex, England

First published in the United States of America by William Morrow & Company, Inc., 1992
Reprinted by arrangement with William Morrow & Company, Inc.
Published in Puffin Books, 1993

1 3 5 7 9 10 8 6 4 2

LIBRARY OF CONGRESS CATALOGING-IN-PUBLICATION DATA
Dygard, Thomas J.
Backfield package / Thomas J. Dygard.    p.    cm.
"First published in the United States of America
by William Morrow & Company, Inc., 1992" — T.p. verso.
Summary: The decision of four high school friends to go to the same
college so that they can continue playing football together is shaken
when one of them begins to receive attention as a star quarterback.
ISBN 0-14-036348-3
[1. Football—Fiction. 2. Friendship—Fiction.
3. High schools—Fiction. 4. Schools—Fiction.] I. Title
[PZ7.D9893Bac    1993]
[Fic]—dc20    93-7721    CIP    AC
Printed in the United States of America

*For my grandson,*
*Adam Nathaniel Stevens,*
*with love*

# Chapter 1

◆        From the beginning, Joe Mitchell liked the idea as much as the rest of them.

The four of them, the backfield of the Hillcrest High Cardinals, would stick together and attend the same college, playing on the same football team for another four years.

The talk had started in the late hours after the final game of their junior season.

The four of them had led the Hillcrest High Cardinals to a 35–7 victory and the championship of the Rend Lake Conference, a league of small high schools in southern Illinois.

Joe Mitchell, the quarterback, had passed for two touchdowns and run for one, capping a season that saw him break both the passing records and the scoring records of Hillcrest High. One of his scoring passes went to Tracy Jackson, the Cardinals' wide receiver. The other went to Coley Brewster, the small but elusive running back. Lew Preston, the powerfully built fullback, plunged for two touchdowns.

It was Hillcrest High's first championship of the Rend Lake Conference in six years, duly celebrated as a historic event in Hillcrest.

There was a party after the game at the high school gym—a jam-packed scene of shouting and cheering—with the four members of the backfield standing together, excited but also a little embarrassed by all the backslapping and handshaking and calls of congratulations.

Then, later, they wound up together in the basement den in Tracy's house with a fire going in the fireplace, talking far into the night.

They were on top of the world—champions—on that night, and they did not want to give up the feeling.

Their talk turned to the future—next year, their senior season. They agreed that the Hillcrest High Cardinals were sure to be champions again. No doubt about it. For one thing, the backfield—the four of them—was returning intact. Beyond that, Charlie Garrison, the center, and Skip Matthews, the right tackle, and others would be returning in the line. No question, the Cardinals were a cinch to repeat as champions of the Rend Lake Conference in their senior year.

But then what?

"We ought to stick together," Coley said. The little running back was sitting cross-legged on the floor, looking around at the other three as he spoke.

"Yeah," Tracy agreed. He turned around from poking at a flaming log in the fireplace. "All four of us go to the same college."

Lew Preston, the biggest and the strongest of the four, a bone-crushing fullback, seldom changed expression. But this time he almost smiled. The idea sounded good to him.

Joe Mitchell, seated on a chair alongside the fireplace, leaned forward with his elbows on his knees and said, "A backfield package, huh? That's us."

"Yeah, man," Coley said with a big grin. "We could room together and everything."

Joe returned Coley's grin. He liked the idea of sticking together in college as much as any of the others. After all, Joe had been throwing a football to Tracy Jackson, the wide receiver, as long as he could remember. He had been sending pitchouts to Coley Brewster, the running back with the funny gait, ever since he first stepped onto a football field. He had been handing off to Lew Preston plunging into the line so long that he knew without thinking precisely where Lew wanted the ball.

They were a good combination, and Joe could

not imagine passing, pitching out, or handing off the football to strangers.

Until this moment, Joe had given little thought to college. His father and mother frequently mentioned that he ought to start thinking about college. But college always seemed so far away, off in the distant future, and there were many other things to think about at Hillcrest High. Now, though, Coley's idea had suddenly put college in a different perspective—a perspective that fit Joe's life. Yes, the four friends could room together, go to classes together, and play in the same backfield for four more years.

"There's bound to be a college that needs a backfield—a whole backfield," Tracy said.

"A whole *championship* backfield," Coley amended.

"Yeah, right," Tracy said.

"Probably one of the smaller schools," Joe said, speaking slowly as he thought through the prospects for the first time.

"Who'd want a big school, anyway?" Coley said. "So many people, you just get lost."

"Yeah, you're right," Joe said. He remembered seeing somewhere the enrollment figures for the University of Illinois up the highway at Champaign—three times as many students as the town of Hillcrest had people. Joe had lived all his life in Hillcrest, comfortable in knowing and being known by everyone. Big numbers were, well, almost scary. He knew his friends felt the same. "Yeah," he added, "you become just a number in a computer."

"Even Southern Illinois University is pretty big," Coley said.

"And too close," Tracy added. "Just twenty or thirty minutes down the road to Carbondale. That'd be like still living at home. I'd rather go away somewhere—not California or Texas, that's too far—but to a place where we could live in a dormitory and all that."

Joe grinned at Tracy. "Yeah, I think so, too." He looked across at Lew, who had been listening quietly, as he usually did. "Okay?" Joe asked.

Lew smiled. "Okay by me."

So the deal was sealed in front of the fireplace in Tracy's den late that night in their junior year when they had won the Rend Lake Conference championship. Yes, they agreed, it was a good idea, the four of them together in college, still going to classes together, sharing living quarters, playing in the same backfield—winning more championships.

By the spring of their junior year, all four of them—and most of the other people in Hillcrest, too—took it for granted that the backfield was going to go from Hillcrest High to a college, intact, as a backfield package.

That's not to say that everyone in Hillcrest agreed that it was a good idea.

Coach Holliman, now in his thirtieth year of teaching biology and coaching football at Hillcrest High, urged caution. "Keep your options open," the veteran coach told the boys. "You can't tell what opportunities might come up for one or the other of you. Don't close any doors just yet. Keep an open mind."

Coach Holliman was stopping short of saying in so many words what some of the townspeople who gathered for mid-morning coffee at Ellie's Cafe on the square were telling one another.

Such as: "Somebody like Illinois or Notre Dame might want Joe Mitchell. He's one fine quarterback, and a good student. But Lew Preston—well, he's a hard-hitting fullback, that's for sure, but he's always had trouble with his grades. College coaches look at that sort of thing."

Or: "Coley Brewster can run circles around anyone, that's true. He jumps around like a little flea and nobody can get a hand on him. But this is high school ball. A college coach is going to take one look at Coley's size and say—no way."

And: "Tracy Jackson can catch any pass thrown within ten yards of him, I know, but let's face it, he's not very fast. These college coaches like speed."

Then, invariably, someone would point out:

"But they've played together all their lives. They're a good combination. They make one another look good. They fit."

Joe and Tracy and Coley and Lew all listened to Coach Holliman's words of caution. And they all agreed, in their own way, that the advice was good: Keep the options open, don't close any doors just yet. Yes, good advice, they felt—for the four of them together, the backfield.

They heard the comments going around town and they shrugged them off—except for one: "They're a good combination. They fit." The four boys liked that one.

There were other comments, too, of a different sort and impossible to shrug off. They were the remarks made at the dinner table in the Mitchell household. The conversation in Coley's living room, and the much shorter exchange in Lew's living room. And the chat between Tracy and his father on the golf course one Saturday afternoon.

The conversations were different from the chatter around town in that they did not touch on the subject of football—not a word about Joe Mitchell's passing and running abilities, Tracy Jackson's pass-catching skills, Coley Brewster's elusive running style, Lew Preston's steamroller strength plunging into the line.

Joe's father and mother talked as if Joe was heading for a trip to the moon, never to return—

and that Coley and Tracy and Lew no longer mattered. "College is a new stage in your life," his father said. "You will be leaving high school, and perhaps your high school friends, behind. You, and your friends, too, will be preparing for careers—different careers, that will be taking you in different directions."

Joe blinked in surprise. He had thought they would understand. But apparently they didn't. He decided not to argue with them—not right now, anyway.

Tracy's father was only a little less alarming. "Son, we'll pick out the college that seems best for you. If your friends choose the same college, okay. But where they go to college is not going to influence our choice."

Tracy gave a little smile and let the statement go by. He usually got his way in the end with his father.

Coley's mother, a widow who taught English at Hillcrest High, raised an eyebrow and said only, "Well, it'll depend on which college. We'll see."

Coley frowned. He saw the possibility of trouble.

Lew's father, a handyman who had not finished high school, expressed surprise. "You're not going to go to work after graduation?" he asked. And that was all.

Comparing notes during a Saturday morning

of fishing at Rend Lake, Coley tried to strike an upbeat chord.

"Your parents didn't say no," he said to Joe, "and neither did my mother." He turned to Tracy. "The closest to a flat-out no was from your dad." Coley gave a little grin and added, "You're usually able to bring him around."

Joe was far from convinced. Something in what his father had said seemed to have an inescapable ring of truth. Maybe his father was right. The four of them were going to go different ways after high school.

Sure, a lot of what Coley said was correct. Coley's mother hadn't said no. She'd just said she was reserving judgment. And, yes, Tracy usually did succeed in getting his way with his father. It remained unsaid, but Lew was not going to have any parental objections—or encouragement.

Joe finally said, "Let's wait and see which schools are offering football scholarships. Then we'll know better where we stand. We'll have something concrete to talk to our parents about."

The three others nodded, each knowing the widely varied needs of the four friends for financial aid.

Tracy did not need a football scholarship. His father, the president of Hillcrest State Bank, could afford to send him to any college he chose.

But Coley surely needed a scholarship to go away to school. His mother was raising Coley and a younger brother alone. Without a scholarship, Coley was headed for the junior college at Maryville, then probably finishing up at Southern Illinois. Joe's parents were prepared to send him to college—they had made this clear the last couple of years—but surely would welcome the financial aid of a football scholarship. Lew had to have a football scholarship. He could not go without one. He was not going to receive any financial aid from home.

With summer, the letters from colleges began arriving—form letters mostly, some with color brochures—asking the boys to consider them for higher education and football. For one reason or another, each boy's name had popped up on one or another college's list of football prospects.

To nobody's surprise, Joe got more letters than any of the others, and he was the only one to receive letters from several major football schools. The letters to Coley, Tracy, and Lew came from state colleges in Illinois and neighboring states, and from small private colleges.

Several colleges sent letters to two of the boys—usually to Joe and one of the others—and a few sent letters to three of them.

In the end, though, only one school—Ryder

State College, located in the town of Ryder in the northeast corner of Indiana—had sent letters to all four of them.

It looked perfect, they agreed. It was a small school, which was what all four boys from the small town of Hillcrest preferred. It was far enough away, but not too far. And, most important, Ryder State wanted all of them.

By the time football practice began in late August for their senior season, and then when classes began in early September, the boys had settled the question: The backfield package was heading for the future at Ryder State.

The boys' parents would agree. They had to.

# Chapter 2

◆ The last Friday night in October was cool and windless, with the arc lights bathing the Hillcrest High football field in a shadowless light. The scoreboard beyond the goalposts at the north end of the field showed: Cardinals 28, Visitors 7. The clock in the center of the scoreboard showed thirty-seven seconds remaining in the game.

The Hillcrest High Cardinals were wrapping up their sixth straight victory since the opening-game loss to the larger Morristown High in a nonconference encounter. Undefeated in Rend Lake Conference play, the Cardinals were taking one more step toward their second consecutive championship.

On the field, Joe broke the huddle and the Cardinals lined up for the final play of the game. Joe, behind the center, scanned the defensive alignment in front of him from force of habit. Then he leaned down and reached under Charlie

Garrison, the center. Joe barked the signals—
"Hut! Hut!"—while the seconds ticked off the
clock. Then he took the snap, clasped the ball to
his stomach with both hands, and fell to the
ground. The clock kept ticking and then the
buzzer sounded, ending the game.

In the wooden bleachers on both sides of the
field, the Hillcrest High fans stood and cheered.

Joe leaped to his feet and, with the others,
raced toward the cheering crowd of Hillcrest
High players at the sideline.

A frowning Coach Holliman passed them, going the other way. He was heading to midfield
for the customary postgame handshake with the
opposing coach. Win or lose, Coach Holliman
frowned all the way through the football season.

Joe met Coach Holliman's scowl with a laugh
and then ran into a bear hug with Lew and some
of the other players just before Coley and Tracy
joined the shouting crowd.

The next morning the four of them gathered
at Tracy's house to wash the copper-colored van
in the circular driveway in front of the large two-
story house. The wash job each weekend was
the small price extracted by Mr. Jackson for
Tracy's use of the van on weekends. The other
three pitched in and helped so they could be on
their way that much earlier.

Their practiced system made short order of

the chore. Lew, the tallest, handled the roof and top edges. Coley did the front end and one side, and Joe the rear and the other side. Tracy washed the wheels and manned the hose for rinsing.

In a matter of minutes, Joe, Coley, and Lew were stepping back, watching Tracy give the final rinsing.

"That's it," Tracy said and walked across to turn off the water. Then he looped the hose into large rings on the grass off the side of the driveway. He would put the hose away in the garage later. He stepped to the front door of the house, opened it, called out, "I'm gone," and closed the door without waiting for an answer.

The four boys piled into the van, Tracy at the wheel, Lew next to him in the front seat, and Joe and Coley in the backseat. Tracy started the engine and pulled away.

"Is your father going to let you take the van off to college?" Coley asked.

"I suppose so," Tracy said, slowing and then stopping at the end of the driveway to glance both ways before pulling out into the street. "Or maybe a new one. This thing is a couple of years old, you know."

Joe glanced ahead and across at his friend at the wheel. If Tracy wanted this van, or a new one, at college, he probably would get it. Tracy usually got what he wanted. Money never seemed to be a problem with the Jackson household. The home of the president of Hillcrest State Bank was one of the largest in Hillcrest, and the copper-colored van was only one of three cars in the Jackson family. Tracy was one of the few at Hillcrest High who always had access to a car.

Joe marveled, as he had before, at the casual way Tracy accepted the van, the large house, the parties at the Hillcrest Country Club—and the casual way Coley and Lew and, yes, Joe himself accepted the fact that Tracy had these things and the rest of them didn't.

There were other differences, too, and they were accepted with equal casualness. For example, Coley, with his mother the English teacher at the controls, made excellent grades, while Lew, with indifferent parents, had terrible classroom problems. Coley probably could get a college scholarship without football. Lew might have trouble gaining entrance despite his ability to crash through the line with a football clutched in both hands.

And Joe? Well, Joe was in the middle. His father managed the Hillcrest Water Works. He earned a solid living. Not the luxury provided by Mr. Jackson, but a comfortable life. Joe's grades were not the match of Coley's, but they were good—good enough to satisfy almost any college entrance requirement.

Where Joe was not in the middle of the group was on the football field. Coley was quick but not strong; Lew was strong but not quick. Joe was quick and strong. Tracy was a step slow going out for a pass or running the ball. Joe was fast in a straightaway run. And Joe was the quarterback, the leader, the player who threw the passes, tossed the pitchouts, and dealt out the handoffs. He was smart on a football field—smart enough that Coach Holliman let him call a lot of the plays on his own.

Together they were, Joe reflected, a backfield package—and friends.

Tracy drove the van the mile and a half from his house to the Hillcrest business district—"the square" with the county courthouse that sided the state highway passing through town, named Main Street along that section of the highway. They cruised Main Street and circled the square and, as always, wound up at Ellie's Cafe. It was where Hillcrest's businesspeople drank their morning coffee during the week, and where the Hillcrest High students hung out on Saturday mornings.

Ellie's Cafe was a spacious place with booths lining one wall and large tables at the front window and in the center of the floor. Smaller tables for two lined the front wall beyond the window. The wall opposite the booths was covered with racks displaying newspapers, magazines, and paperback books. The major fixture of the place was Ellie herself, a huge woman with gray hair tied back in a bun, manning her station at the cash register.

The boys walked through, acknowledging the occasional call of congratulations—"Nice game," "Nice running, Coley," "Good game, Joe"—and took seats around one of the large tables near the rear. Tracy and Coley ordered soft drinks, and Joe and Lew each ordered a glass of milk. Then the four of them set about the business of deciding what to do on this Saturday.

For Coley and Lew, the afternoon was booked with part-time jobs. Coley would be behind the soda fountain at Wiggams' Drug Store across the square. Lew would be working with his father on some handyman project. Tracy was scheduled for golf with his father at Hillcrest Country Club. Joe, with the others occupied, would probably watch the Notre Dame–Southern Cal football game on television with his father.

Two girls came through the door and took seats at one of the smaller tables. One of them was Barbara Lanford, a pretty blonde with blue eyes who played on the Hillcrest High tennis team in the spring. She and Joe played tennis together occasionally. She was quick, strong, and tough on a tennis court.

Looking around, Barbara spotted Joe and gave a little wave, and then got up and walked toward the boys' table.

Approaching, Barbara had the look on her face of someone with something more to say than the casual "nice game" greeting after a victory, and Joe waited with a questioning look on his face.

She shook her head, declining the chair Joe had pulled out for her. "I'm with Marilyn," she said. She glanced quickly at the other boys and seemed to arrive at a decision. If she had been intending to say or ask something, she now changed her mind. "Good game last night," she said finally.

Joe, feeling a little puzzled, watched her a moment, wondering if she had something more to say. The other boys remained silent, apparently sharing the feeling that she had come over with something on her mind other than a compliment on the football victory. Finally, Joe asked, "Want to play some tennis this afternoon?"

"I can't today. How about tomorrow?"

Joe glanced at his friends. None of them said anything. "Sure," he said.

"Good," Barbara said. "It'll probably do you good to lose at something for a change."

Joe grinned at her. "We'll see."

Half an hour later, the Hillcrest High backfield had left Ellie's Cafe after making a few decisions.

First, they would go to Happy Andy's out on the highway north of town for hamburgers for lunch. Then they would part and regroup in the evening to drive over to Carbondale for a new horror film.

The next day the backfield package began to unravel for Joe Mitchell.

The place was unlikely: the municipal tennis courts in McDermott Park on the edge of Hillcrest, out by Lake Hillcrest.

And the person whose casual remark started the unraveling was an unlikely candidate for the role: Barbara Lanford.

"I heard your name mentioned at Randolph University this week," Barbara said.

They were seated on a bench at the side of the court, taking a breather after their first set. The weather was warm and sunny on this fourth Sunday in October—unusually warm for so late in the season—and both were perspiring. Joe had eked out victory, 6–4, 5–7, 6–4. Now he was wiping his face with a towel.

Joe turned to Barbara. "Me? At Randolph University?"

Joe knew about Randolph. Everyone did. The Randolph Tigers were a perennial college football power. They were always in the rankings, always beating teams from Alabama to UCLA, always ending their season in a bowl game. Randolph was a large university located in the hills of central Tennessee. Joe knew, too, what the school and its setting looked like. Randolph had been one of the schools sending Joe, and only Joe of the four friends, a brochure and a letter asking him to consider applying and playing football. He had dropped the brochure and the letter—only a form letter, actually—in the drawer of his bureau with the other letters from other schools. Randolph was one of those big schools that put him off a little. Besides, the backfield was sticking together. Joe had little use for an inquiry that went to him alone, and not to the others.

But now, what was this all about?

"My parents and I, we were down there on Thursday," Barbara said. "You know, just looking the place over."

Joe was aware that Barbara and her parents had been visiting campuses around the Midwest. Like Joe, Barbara was a senior, and she was trying to decide on a college. For Barbara, money was not a factor in the choice. The daughter of the principal owner of Lanford Mall, halfway between Hillcrest and Carbondale, did not have any financial worries.

"And . . ." Joe said.

"Well, we were at this little reception at the end of the tour—about a dozen kids from all over, with their parents—and this man came up and started talking. He knew we were from Hillcrest, and he asked if we knew you."

"Really? Who was he?"

"I don't remember his name. I'm not even sure he said it. But he did say he was with the athletic department." She paused and then, as if suddenly remembering a detail, said, "And . . . oh, yes, he said he had seen you play. Did you know that somebody from Randolph had come to one of the Cardinals' games to watch you play?"

"You're kidding."

"That's what he said. He also said that you were on their 'most-wanted' list." She smiled and added, "Sounds like you robbed a bank, doesn't it?"

Joe, frowning, shook his head in silence. He stared straight ahead. The two kids banging a ball around on the far court went out of focus. "I'm really surprised," he said finally, immediately deciding that that sounded like a dumb statement. But it was the truth.

"I started to tell you about this—or, rather, ask you about it—yesterday morning in Ellie's," Barbara said. "But then it suddenly dawned on me that the man didn't ask about anyone but you, and I thought maybe . . ." She let the sentence trail off.

"Yeah," Joe said, understanding. "But I've never talked to anyone from Randolph. I got a letter or two from them last summer. Just routine form letters, you know, saying they hoped I'd consider Randolph and stuff like that. I got the same kinds of letters from several schools. We all did. Nothing special." He shook his head. "This is strange."

"Did the others get letters from Randolph?"

Joe looked at her. "No," he said. "That was one reason I didn't pay much attention, that and the fact that they were such form letters. I figured that some computer just spewed out a lot of names of people who were going to be graduating and they sent a letter to all the names." He paused. "But you said this man said he came to see me play?"

"Yes."

Joe stared out across the tennis courts. He got the two kids on the far court in focus. They were calling it quits, putting the balls into a canvas bag. Joe's thoughts went back to those few brief moments when he had thought that maybe— yes, maybe—he could play for a major college football team. But the thought was always followed by a question: Who would ever notice Joe Mitchell at tiny Hillcrest High? But now . . .

And what about the backfield package? What would the others say? The world suddenly seemed full of problems.

Barbara broke the long silence. "This man asked my father all sorts of questions about you."

"Oh? Like what?"

"What kind of a reputation you had around town and at school, what kind of a student you were—that sort of thing."

"Umm."

Barbara grinned at Joe. "Don't worry. My father didn't tell him a thing." She got to her feet. "Are you ready to go again?"

Joe did not feel like grinning back at her small joke. "Sure," he said absently, and got up and walked onto the court.

She beat him, 6–3, 6–3, in their second set.

# Chapter 3

By the time Joe had dropped off Barbara at home and driven the mile to his house, he felt like his brain had been turned inside out.

He had played through the second set on the tennis court in a daze, trying to concentrate on reaching and then returning the rifle shots Barbara was sending across the net. He played like an automaton, wishing the set would end.

Driving her home, he had managed with great effort to keep up a line of chatter with a smile frozen on his face. To his relief, the conversation did not include any mention of Randolph University. They talked about next week's Mount Holly game, Mrs. Walker's very tough grading system in her calculus class, a trip Barbara and her parents were going to make to Northwestern University in Evanston—but not, thankfully, someone at Randolph University inquiring about Joe Mitchell.

After letting Barbara out at her home, Joe no longer needed to smile and chatter, and he drove the car with a deepening frown on his face, both hands clutching the steering wheel. His world, always so settled, seemed to be whirling, and his mind was having trouble keeping up with the crazy turn of events.

Wasn't he going to go to Ryder State with his friends? Sure, no question. That was what he wanted. Wasn't it? Sure. So, who cared about Randolph University? Yeah, who?

When he pulled into the driveway at his home, he realized that he had no recollection of the drive from Barbara's house. His mind had been churning with other thoughts. With a slight feeling of alarm, he hoped he had not absently driven through any stop signs.

He got out of the car, remembered he had left the keys, and opened the door again and reached in to get them.

His father was in the front yard, giving the annual autumnal pruning to the flowering plum tree. He grinned at Joe and said, "She beat you. I can see it on your face."

"Yeah." Joe nodded and managed a small smile, and walked toward the front door.

Joe went inside the house, called out, "Home," for the benefit of his mother, and then took the stairs two at a time heading for his room. He closed the door and walked across to the bureau drawer where he kept the letters he had received from schools during the summer. He had not looked at the letters in weeks.

He opened the bureau drawer and lifted out the dozen or so letters, then sat down on the edge of his bed. He sifted through the papers until he had separated the two letters from Randolph, and the brochure, from the others.

He reread the two Randolph letters.

The first one, for sure, was a form letter. It congratulated him on heading into his senior year, as if that were a big deal. The letter then congratulated him on his accomplishments on the football field—without saying what the accomplishments were. The letter assumed he was going to college. It explained that Randolph University was an outstanding educational institution with a great football program and a great tradition, located in the beautiful hill country of central Tennessee. Yes, purely a form letter.

The second letter, though, mentioned the possibility of a visit to the Randolph campus after the end of football season. "To meet the coaching staff and see the beautiful campus and the outstanding athletic facilities," the letter said. The invitation to visit, Joe thought, lifted the letter out of the ordinary, put it somewhere beyond the routine. Funny, it hadn't struck him that way when he received it last summer. But, then, the only important question at that time had been: Had Coley, Tracy, and Lew received letters from Randolph University?

But now Joe frowned slightly and thought that yes, visiting Randolph University might be a good thing to do.

He looked up from the letter and his frown deepened. He would be making the visit alone, without his friends. He would have to move away from his three friends, leave them behind, to visit Randolph. He could see in his mind the expressions on their faces. The questions would be clear even before anyone spoke. Why was he visiting Randolph University? They were all going to Ryder State together, weren't they?

Joe looked at the brochure. There were color photographs of the campus with hills in the background. There was an aerial shot of the huge football stadium, filled to capacity, on a sunny afternoon. He had seen that stadium on television more than once, watching the Randolph Tigers play Tennessee or LSU or somebody.

Could Joe Mitchell play quarterback for that team in that stadium?

Again the word "alone" came into his mind. Playing quarterback for the Randolph Tigers would mean playing without his friends in the backfield.

Joe laid the brochure on the bed alongside the letters.

He wondered about attending a huge school, living on a mammoth campus, being just one of thousands and thousands of students. It would be strange, maybe even frightening. But Randolph University was a prestigious school. Everyone had heard of it, even those who did not care about football. Joe knew that his father and mother would like the idea of seeing their son attend Randolph.

One phrase relayed by Barbara kept popping back into his mind: most-wanted list.

What exactly did that mean?

Well, Joe thought, it meant that Randolph University really wanted Joe Mitchell, quarterback of the Hillcrest High Cardinals. That's what it meant. But too bad about your friends, Joe.

It meant something else, too, Joe thought. He picked up the stack of letters and glanced through them. He noted the names of the schools. Some of the letters came from other major universities, the likes of Randolph University. Maybe he was on other most-wanted lists at other schools and just didn't know about it. Other schools, whose letters he had dropped in the drawer and forgotten because they had not sent letters to Coley, Tracy, and Lew.

Joe reflected that he might be hearing from Randolph University again after the end of football season. Yes, probably so. They had mentioned a visit. They would be writing to follow up. And he might hear again from other schools, too. What was he going to tell them? Was he going to say, "Thanks but no thanks," or . . . ?

Joe dropped the letters back on the bed. He sat motionless a moment, then took a deep breath.

He could hardly believe that Randolph University—the Randolph Tigers—had sent someone all the way from Tennessee to southern Illinois to see him play—Joe Mitchell of the Hillcrest High Cardinals.

But that was what the man had told the Lanfords, so it must be true. Joe wondered which game the man had seen.

And did that mean that other schools, without saying anything, had sent someone to watch him play? Maybe so. Maybe there was going to be a college scout in the stands when the Cardinals played at Mount Holly next Friday night.

Joe stood up and walked over to the window. He stared out at the long shadows cast by the late-afternoon sun across his backyard. He had been looking out this window all his life. Was he going to be seeing the world from the backfield of the Ryder State Eagles, or . . . ?

From the moment Barbara had started talking about Randolph, Joe had felt a mixture of surprise, confusion, and, yes, excitement. He and

Coley and Tracy and Lew were going to Ryder State College together. Ryder State, and only Ryder State, was interested in all four of them. So it was Ryder State. Simple, huh?

But now Randolph University was interested in him, really, seriously interested. And maybe others were, too.

And, to his horror, Joe liked the idea.

Joe leaned into the stairwell and called out to his mother: "Do I have time for a shower before dinner?"

"Thirty minutes," she called back.

He stood in the shower, letting the hot water wash away the sweat of the tennis match. But the hot water did not wash away the questions in Joe's mind, nor the faces of Coley, Tracy, and Lew, which kept appearing in front of his eyes.

"Say, fellows, meant to tell you earlier, but this major school is interested in me, but not you, and so—so long." Joe almost flinched at the thought.

Coley would shout his protest. Joe could hear the word: "Wha-a-a-t?" Tracy's jaw would drop in speechless astonishment. Lew's expression would not change, and he would not say anything, but somehow a feeling of betrayal would show through.

They were his friends, his teammates of four

years' standing. He had won with them, and he had lost with them. He had laughed and cheered with them, and he had cried—actually cried once—with them. How could he do this to them?

How?

Joe turned slowly in the shower, giving himself a last rinsing, and then stepped out onto the bathmat and reached for a towel.

At dinner, Joe said nothing to his parents about what Barbara had told him. He did not want to talk about it. Not yet. Later, for sure, but not now. Probably his father was going to hear about it around town in the next few days. Barbara and her parents were certain to tell people. And then Joe's father would mention it to him. That way, Joe could shrug it off, smile it away to his parents as just another piece of gossip clattering through the Hillcrest grapevine. That would buy him some time to think.

Joe and his parents were seated at the large round table in the bay window off the kitchen, the site of most of the meals in the Mitchell household.

Joe's father was saying something about the Mount Holly defensive backs. He had received a report on the Green Wave from a man at the Hillcrest Water Works who had gone to Mount

Holly to look at a new filtration system being installed. The Mount Holly defensive backs, it seemed, were pretty good.

Joe ate a piece of fried chicken and watched his father, pretending to listen.

He knew that his father and mother would be pleased by any indication that the backfield package was breaking up, that Joe, or any of them, appeared to be pulling out. They did not object to Coley or Tracy or Lew. They had no argument with the four of them going to the same school. And they accepted the fact that Joe wanted to play football in college.

But Joe was well aware that they did not want the idea of football or the four of them sticking together to become the determining factor in Joe's choice of a college.

Through all the talk of Ryder State, his father and mother always responded with a vagueness that Joe recognized. They were not protesting, but they were not accepting, either. He heard a lot of, "We'll see," and, "There's time to decide," and "It's a possibility you may want to look into." It was their way of trying to lead Joe into making the right decision on his own. Joe had seen the procedure in action before. Also, he knew, they were holding off any pressure until the Hillcrest High football season was over, and Joe appreciated their consideration.

Maybe they're right, Joe thought, in holding

off endorsing his plans to go to Ryder State with his friends. He recalled the color photograph of the Randolph campus in the brochure. Maybe he should look around.

But this wasn't the time to mention Randolph University as a possibility. Not the time to mention the possible end of the backfield package. Not now, with three important games remaining to be played.

Joe needed time to think, to sort out the troubling thoughts circling in his mind.

If he was going to do some looking around on his own—at Randolph and maybe at some other schools—he was going to have to let Coley and Tracy and Lew know that he was no longer so sure about Ryder State. But he did not have to do that until the season was over. He had three more weeks, at least. Maybe it wouldn't hurt to start giving out some small advance signals, though. That way, if he went his own way, it wouldn't come as such a big surprise. He could say, in a casual way, that he wasn't so sure about Ryder State, after all. Yes, that sounded good. But—no, no, no. He clamped his jaw and decided that nothing—*nothing*—needed to be said right away. Certainly not for three weeks, when the Mount Holly and Marianna and Hoytville games would be behind them. Plenty of time after that.

"What do you think?" his father asked.

"Huh?"

"You weren't listening."

"I'm sorry. I was thinking about something else."

Joe's mother was looking at him in a funny way. "Is anything wrong?" she asked.

Joe rolled his eyes to the ceiling. His mother could spot trouble in his world a mile away. "No, there's nothing wrong," he said. "I was just thinking about something." He looked back at his father. "I'm sorry. What were you saying?"

"Just that it looks like the Mount Holly secondary might be the toughest you've faced since Morristown. You may have some trouble getting your passes through them."

Joe grinned at his father. "Ah, in that case we'll just run Lew up the middle," he said.

## Chapter 4

◆         The Hillcrest grapevine was slow in picking up on the story.

Maybe Barbara Lanford was telling girl-friends that someone at Randolph University had asked about Joe Mitchell. But that in itself was not a hot news story. After all, everyone at Hillcrest High knew that most of the senior football players had received letters from one school or another. And everyone knew that Joe Mitchell had received a handful, some of them from big schools. So what?

More important, Barbara's father spent his days in his office and in the lobbies and shops of Lanford Mall outside of town. He was not one of those gathering for the morning coffee sessions at Ellie's Cafe on the square. So the hub of the Hillcrest grapevine never received the report at all.

As for Joe, he said nothing to anyone.

Not that Joe was worried about the story getting out. He knew what his response was going to be. If somebody asked about it, he was going to smile and say, "Oh." That was all. Nothing else. Or, if the teller knew that Barbara had already told Joe about it, he was going to say, "Yeah, that's what I heard." Just that. Nothing more.

But what did concern Joe was the very real possibility that someone—particularly Coley or Tracy or Lew—would get the impression he was taking the report from Randolph University seriously.

Then the trouble would start.

Was Joe Mitchell pulling out of the backfield package? Was Joe going to Randolph? Alone, without the others? On the Hillcrest grapevine, that would be big news.

First Coley, and then the rest of them, would demand—well, ask for, if not actually insist on—reassurances from Joe that he was not tempted to pull out of the backfield package.

All along, one or the other of them had been asking for reaffirmation from the rest. In an indirect way, to be sure, but asking, nevertheless. Coley or one of the others would say something like, "When we're at Ryder State, we'll do it this way, right?" And then wait for the others to say, "Right." And that was the same as saying, "Yeah, sure, we're all going to Ryder State together. The deal is still on."

Joe did not want to be pressed for reassurances—not for three weeks, anyway, until the Cardinals were past the last game. The Cardinals needed to have everything normal, upbeat, and uncluttered to defeat the three remaining teams on the schedule. And the Cardinals had to defeat them to win their second straight Rend Lake Conference championship.

Joe knew that, if pressed, he could not lie to his friends. He would have to level with them. He would have to tell them that he was having second thoughts about Ryder State. He would have to say that he was planning to do some looking around at other, bigger schools.

Yet, he could not tell them that and still hope to have the backfield clicking at top form against Mount Holly and Marianna and Hoytville. An angry Coley, a disappointed Tracy, a betrayed Lew—those were not the ingredients a quarterback needed with him in the backfield.

So Joe braced himself to deliver an easy smile and a casual answer when the inevitable questions popped up—casual enough, he hoped, to forestall any need for reassurances from his friends.

Later, after the end of the season, he would be able to explain. And his friends would be able to understand why he felt he had to look into all opportunities. Sure, Joe would say, he might still wind up going to Ryder State with them.

But he would be foolish to turn his back on other possibilities without even looking and listening. His friends would understand. They would have to understand.

Joe realized, almost with a feeling of shock, that his conclusion added up to the same advice that his father and, yes, Coach Holliman, too, had been giving him all along. It took Barbara's story about Randolph University to bring everything into focus for him. Joe did need to look around at all the possibilities. And if one of those other possibilities looked best for Joe Mitchell, well, his friends would just have to understand.

But would they understand? Joe could hear Coley's wail: "But what about our deal, all of us sticking together?"

For all his brooding, Joe could not think of a reply that would satisfy either him or his friends.

But, then, maybe he would never need to come up with a reply. Maybe Randolph, in fact, was not all that interested in Joe Mitchell. Maybe everyone was on the most-wanted list. Maybe it was just a recruiting ploy to make sure that every prospect gave at least a second look to Randolph. That could be it. Joe might find in the end that Randolph had six quarterbacks on the most-wanted list. And maybe the other big schools were all doing the same thing.

No, maybe Joe wouldn't have to answer

Coley's wailing question, Tracy's unbelieving look, Lew's feeling of betrayal.

Maybe there was nothing to worry about.

Maybe.

Joe tried to put it all out of his mind as he went through the day—classes in the morning, lunch in the cafeteria with his friends, classes in the afternoon, and then the walk with Tracy from the last class to the dressing room to change for practice.

"My dad says he hears that Mount Holly's got the toughest secondary that we've seen," Joe said to Tracy as they went down the stairs toward the basement.

Tracy laughed. "Then we'll give the ball to Lew up the middle," he said.

"That's what I told my dad."

They reached the bottom of the stairs and turned into the dressing room, already full of players changing into pads, sweatshirts, cleated shoes.

Coach Holliman, his frown firmly fixed in place, was pacing around the room, trying to determine if anyone was missing.

Joe and Tracy walked across to their lockers. Coley and Lew were already in front of their lockers, half dressed for the drill.

By this hour on Monday, Joe was a little sur-

prised that there were no signs that the Lanfords'
story was making the rounds of Hillcrest and
the corridors of Hillcrest High. He gave Coley a
questioning look. Had his friend heard the
story? Was he going to ask Joe about it?

But Coley just grinned, and Joe managed a
smile in return and began unbuttoning his shirt.

Out on the practice field, Coach Holliman
called the squad around him at the sideline before sending the players into their warm-up cal-
isthenics.

"Mount Holly has lost three games," he said,
"but don't be lulled into overconfidence." He
turned slowly, frowning at the circle of players.
"Their losses came early in the season, and one
of them to a much larger school. Mount Holly
has been improving steadily all season long.
They're a good football team now. It is going to
take one of your best games to beat them."

And then he sounded a note that all the players
had heard before: "And to play your best game,
you're going to have to have your best practice
week ever."

The Monday drill, as always, was a light one.
There was passing, running, kicking. There were
signal drills for the backfield and blocking drills
for the linemen. But there was no contact—no
jarring tackles, no jolting blocks.

At the finish, Coach Holliman announced,
"Tomorrow we scrimmage."

As Joe was jogging off the field toward the school building and the locker room in the basement, he heard the coach call his name. He slowed and turned, and then stopped, waiting for Coach Holliman to stride up even with him.

Joe was half expecting a warning about the Mount Holly defensive backs, whom his father had mentioned. Or maybe the coach just wanted to issue a general word of caution about overconfidence.

But Coach Holliman said, "Joe, the *St. Louis Journal-Gazette* is preparing a story on college football prospects on the high school teams in the area. They called me about you."

"Oh?"

The *St. Louis Journal-Gazette* was the morning newspaper for all the small towns of southern Illinois. It was regular reading in the Mitchell household, along with the *Hillcrest Light*, published in the afternoon.

"The story will be appearing in a week or so, I guess," Coach Holliman said.

They walked together for a few steps without speaking. It struck Joe as strange for Coach Holliman to concern himself about a newspaper story, whether by Harry Beard of the *Hillcrest Light* or a stranger at the St. Louis paper. Clearly, Coach Holliman had something more to say.

But it was Joe who broke the silence. "And

the others?" he asked, assuming that Coley and Tracy and Lew qualified as college prospects. "Do they know about it yet?"

Coach Holliman understood the question. "You're the only one on our team that the sportswriter asked about," he said.

Joe blinked. Like Randolph University. Interested in Joe, and only Joe. But he said nothing.

"That's why I wanted to mention it to you. Just don't be surprised when the story appears."

"Uh-huh."

"And don't be impressed, either. It's just a sportswriter's opinion."

Joe turned to Coach Holliman with a small grin on his face, but the coach was already angling away from Joe to intercept some player who, undoubtedly, needed to be told his practice session had not been good enough.

Tracy, as usual, was the last one dressed, and Joe, Coley, and Lew stood in the corridor waiting for him.

"Why does it always have to take him so long?" Joe asked.

"He spends a lot of time combing his hair," Coley said with a laugh.

Joe did not join in the laugh.

"Here he comes," Lew said.

"Ready?" Tracy said as he approached.

Joe almost snorted.

"No," Coley said with an expression of mock seriousness on his face. "Would you mind waiting a few minutes for me?"

"Huh?" said Tracy. Then he caught on. "Oh."

For Joe, Coley's lighthearted remarks came as a relief. Coley did not joke when something serious was weighing on his mind. The easy banter was one more bit of evidence that Coley had not heard about Randolph University's threat to the backfield package. Joe was not going to have to answer any probing questions on the walk home. With luck, he would not even be called upon to deliver another of the occasional statements of reassurance.

The four of them headed down the corridor, and Joe saw Coach Holliman walking toward them, going from his office to the locker room. All but the stragglers had left. Tracy frequently was among the players caught by the coach in his daily check, so they all knew Coach Holliman's cutting remarks to the slow dressers. To Tracy he usually said, "Just like I tell you on the field, Jackson, you ought to be faster." Coach Holliman liked everything done quickly, with no wasted motion, both on and off the field.

Tonight the coach passed them with a simple, "Good night, boys."

As the coach walked past, Joe wondered if he had heard the Lanfords' story. It was possible, even likely. People in Hillcrest frequently called the coach when they heard something—good or bad—about one of the players. But if the coach had heard, he was giving no indication. Maybe he, like Joe, wanted to keep distractions quietly out of sight in the face of three important games.

The boys walked out the double doors and crossed the gravel parking lot in the deepening dusk of the early evening. By now, in late October, it was almost dark at six o'clock. But the cold weather still had not moved in. They took a left at the street and headed out on the eight blocks they would walk together before peeling off in different directions for the last blocks to their houses.

At his house, Joe called out his usual greeting—"Home"—as he closed the front door behind him.

His mother replied with her usual response, "We're in the kitchen."

But when Joe arrived in the kitchen, after dropping his jacket and books on a chair in the living room, his father did not ask his usual question: "How was practice?"

Instead, he said, "Harold Lanford called me today."

# Chapter 5

◆ Joe responded to the coach as planned—a shrug, a smile, the perfect picture of indifference to the story going around. "Yeah, Barbara told me what the guy said when we were playing tennis." Joe tried hard to sound casual.

But it didn't work.

His father listened, tilted his head slightly, and waited. Just waited.

Joe took another stab. "Look," he said, "it doesn't necessarily mean anything. These big football schools send letters to everybody. They've got hundreds of names on their lists. I'm just one of the names."

"Harold Lanford didn't get that impression."

"What does Mr. Lanford know?"

Mr. Mitchell leaned forward. "Harold Lanford said that what the man said was nothing compared with the way he said it. He left no doubt that they are very interested in you, and this was not just some chatter at a reception."

The statement surprised Joe. Mr. Lanford had conveyed something that Barbara hadn't. Maybe being on the most-wanted list meant something after all. Joe was tempted to say, "Really?" He wanted to hear more. But he said nothing.

Instead, Joe took a deep breath, then dropped into a chair next to his father at the table in the bay window. On the other side of the kitchen, his mother did something with a couple of knobs on the stove and then walked across and sat at the table.

Joe watched her, then looked back at his father. He was going to have to talk about it. He didn't want to. There were too many new thoughts still swirling around in his mind, waiting to be sorted out. He wasn't ready to talk. But the time had come. There was no escape.

He gave a little shrug. Maybe now was as good a time as any. Maybe, even, talking would help.

"Look," Joe said, and then stopped. He realized he did not know what he wanted to say next.

His mother picked up the statement. "Yes, let's look at it," she said. "Randolph University is an outstanding school. It's the kind of school your dad and I would have chosen for you. And, in addition, it seems Randolph is interested in you as a football player. You've always said you wanted to play ball in college."

Mr. Mitchell said, "Joe, this has all the makings of a really great opportunity for you, an opportunity you shouldn't let go by without looking at it very carefully."

Joe nodded, staring at a spot on the far side of the tabletop. His parents were, as always, trying to guide him toward the decision they considered the right one, instead of coming down hard with a flat set of orders. Joe understood.

But they were making it sound like Coley and Tracy and Lew did not exist, or did not matter. He saw in his mind the faces of his friends and, to his alarm, the faces seemed far away, off in the distance and blurred. He frowned.

His father, seeming to read the frown correctly, spoke. "But you find it very difficult to think about telling Coley and Tracy and Lew that you may go your own way, that you may have a marvelous opportunity that they don't have. Right?"

Joe looked up at his father. "Something like that," he said.

"Joe, you are going to be finishing high school and moving on in life. You are going to have to leave high school behind, and perhaps leave Hillcrest behind. And sometimes in order to do that, you have to leave Hillcrest High friends behind. You are moving on in life, to other friends in other places."

"I know. I know. But . . ."

"But it's hard," his mother said.

Joe looked at his mother. "Yes," he said. Then he turned back to his father. He hesitated. Finally, he said, "For a year all we've talked about is sticking together—the backfield package. I can't just . . ."

His father was nodding as Joe spoke. Then, when Joe let the sentence trail off, he said, "Maybe you won't have to."

"What?"

"Willard Jackson may not want his son to attend Ryder State just so he can continue to play football with his friends. Mr. Jackson can send Tracy to any school in the country. He may have plans that we don't know about. And then there's Lew. You know that he has trouble with his grades. He may not be able to gain entrance. And Coley—I don't know—but maybe Mrs. Brewster has ideas of her own."

"Uh-huh, I know," Joe said. And he did know that what his father said might be true. But none of them—Tracy, Coley, Lew—had shown any signs of pulling out of the deal. So how could Joe do it?

"There's no need to do anything right now. So let's wait and see. And not close any doors. Okay?"

"Sure."

Joe made a move to get up, the conversation

at an end. But his father's glance at his mother stopped him. There was more to come. Joe waited.

"I spoke to Coach Holliman early this afternoon, after Harold Lanford called me."

"You called Coach Holliman?"

"Yes."

"He knows about this Randolph University thing, then?"

"Yes. He already knew about it. I wasn't giving him any news."

More to himself than to his parents, Joe said, "He knew before practice today."

"Yes."

"Funny, he didn't say anything at practice," Joe said. "And I walked part of the way in with him after practice."

"He wants to talk to you tomorrow."

"About what? About Randolph?"

"Yes."

Joe bristled. He'd listened to his parents. Now he was going to have to listen to Coach Holliman. He, Joe, had to figure out the solution. Joe shook his head. He said, "I don't see—"

"You're going to be interested in what he has to say," his father said.

"Oh? What is it?"

"I agreed with him that it is better for him to tell you."

"Look, if he's just going to lecture me—"

"He's not, Joe. Wait and hear him out."

Joe looked at his father. He had the feeling he was being tugged at from one direction by his friends, from another direction by his parents—and now from yet a third direction by Coach Holliman.

Then he turned to his mother. "When do we eat?" he asked.

The quicker he finished dinner, the quicker he could get to his room, close the door, and—to his relief—be alone.

The study hall period on Tuesday morning was barely five minutes old when the door opened and Sarah Hunt came in and walked across to Mrs. Henderson's desk. Sarah was one of the students who spent one period a day clerking in the principal's office, picking up attendance records, running errands, and doing some filing. Sarah laid a note in front of Mrs. Henderson.

The teacher read the note, then looked up and found Joe. She glared at Joe a moment, then motioned him to her desk.

"Come right back here afterward," she said to Joe.

"I will."

Joe followed Sarah out of the study hall into the corridor and said, "I know the way."

"I have to bring you," Sarah said. "It's the rules."

Joe shrugged and walked with her the familiar path to Coach Holliman's office, a small cubicle off the corridor alongside the locker room. Sarah walked on, returning to the principal's office, and Joe stepped into the open doorway of the football coach's office and stopped.

"Come in, Joe." Coach Holliman was seated at his old green metal desk. He was frowning up at Joe. "Have a seat." He gestured at the one wooden chair in front of the desk.

Joe sat down and waited.

Coach Holliman looked at him a moment, then abruptly got up and walked around the desk and closed the door. He returned to his seat behind the desk.

"I was hoping this wouldn't come up until the season was over," Coach Holliman said. "The last thing a quarterback needs going into three important games is distraction."

"I'll be okay," Joe said.

The coach stared at Joe and then said, "Yes, I'm sure you will." He watched Joe for another moment before speaking. "But with this Randolph story going around town, there's something you should know before Coley and Tracy and Lew start asking questions."

Joe's right eyebrow went up a notch. He knew the coach was aware of their plan to stick together. Everyone in Hillcrest knew about it. But Joe was surprised to find that Coach Holliman might understand the pressures his friends might exert on him, demanding reassurances that the deal still remained in place.

Coach Holliman leaned back in his chair. He picked a pencil off the desk, and then laid it back down. "Andy Abrams, the head coach at Randolph University, is an old college teammate of mine. We played together at Iowa. He played guard and I played tackle, side by side."

Joe frowned slightly. This did not sound like what he was expecting. Something was going on. But what? He did not know. But he had a funny feeling, a mix of fear and excitement, that forces beyond his control were starting to influence his life. Was that good? He did not know. He waited for Coach Holliman to continue.

"I called Andy last summer and suggested that he might want to send you a letter or two expressing interest, and that he might want to send someone to take a look at you."

Joe blinked in surprise. "You did?"

"Yes, I did. Andy told me that he would put you on the list." Coach Holliman paused. "I haven't heard from him since. There are very strict rules governing college coaches contacting high school football prospects, and I'm sure Andy is very careful to avoid violating them. But it seems clear now that he did send someone to look at you, and that someone was very impressed."

Coach Holliman's familiar frown faded, to be replaced by a small smile.

"As for a man approaching the Lanfords at the reception at Randolph, well, I'd guess it was no accident. Andy Abrams is a pretty smart fellow, always was. He probably has someone routinely check the names and addresses of prospective students signed up for a campus tour. If there's a football player among them, he has somebody from his staff on hand. In this case, it seems, just the fact that there was somebody from Hillcrest, anybody from Hillcrest, was enough."

"He was there just to ask about me?"

Coach Holliman nodded. "To do two things, I think. First, it gave them a chance to ask someone other than your coach about you—and to ask not just about your football ability but about what kind of a young man you are." He paused. "And it gave them an opportunity to send a message back to you that Randolph is really very interested, without breaking any of the recruiting rules."

Joe looked past Coach Holliman, through the window, out across the parking lot, and toward the house across the street. His thoughts whirled around in his head. So it's for real. The most-wanted list is important. Randolph is truly interested in Joe Mitchell. Does this make things easier? No, tougher. The faces of his three friends appeared in his thoughts. Then the picture of

Randolph's football stadium, packed with fans, with Joe Mitchell playing quarterback.

Finally, Joe said, speaking barely above a whisper, "I see."

Coach Holliman's frown was back in place, the small grin gone. "I'm telling you all this for two reasons. One, I think it is important for you to understand that Randolph is truly serious about you, and that you should not discard the idea out of hand. And, second, Joe, I am a teacher as well as a coach, and my advice to you is to give serious consideration to such an outstanding school."

Joe nodded. There had been no mention of Coley, Tracy, and Lew, no mention of their deal to stick together. And Joe did not mention his friends or their agreement now. He said, "That's about the same thing my father and mother have told me."

Coach Holliman watched Joe a minute. Joe thought the coach was going to say something about the backfield package. But instead he said, "There's nothing to be done before December first. That is when college coaches may contact you, and when you may visit a school as their guest. So there is no point in letting this business distract you or any of the others during the next three weeks."

Joe shook his head and mumbled, almost to himself, "Yes, the others."

"You'll want to give some thought to what you're going to say when Coley and Tracy and Lew ask about Randolph."

"Sure."

Joe returned to Mrs. Henderson's study hall.

Joe had no trouble keeping his mind on the Mount Holly Green Wave during the football practice sessions that followed. The rough contact, the intense concentration, the sheer physical exertions on the practice field left no room for wondering about keeping options open, or sticking to a deal with your friends.

The classroom, the lunch periods, and the time at home, though, were something different.

Joe caught himself dreaming of quarterbacking for the Randolph Tigers in a major game before a stadium packed with thousands and a television audience numbering in the millions. He saw himself on New Year's Day taking the field—where?—in the Sugar Bowl in New Orleans, the Cotton Bowl in Dallas, the Orange Bowl in Miami. He would be famous and happy. His father and mother would be pleased that he was going to graduate from Randolph University.

Then he saw himself alone on an enormous campus without his friends. From there the picture moved easily to the four of them together at Ryder State, going to classes together, living together, playing together in the backfield, winning games, being together.

Coley, Tracy, and Lew did indeed hear about the Lanfords' encounter at Randolph University, and they did ask about it—but not until Wednesday at lunch.

Coley did the asking. "Barbara said someone at Randolph was asking her family about you," he said. He spoke matter-of-factly, but the look in his eyes was troubling to Joe. Coley's steady gaze seemed to come across as an accusation.

Tracy and Lew said nothing, watching Joe and waiting with Coley for his reply.

Joe, glancing from one to the other of them, guessed that they had talked about it among themselves earlier and now wanted to hear what Joe had to say. For the first time ever, Joe had the uncomfortable feeling that it was the one of him against the three of them.

Finally, Joe shrugged and said, "Yeah, that's what Barbara told me the other day."

"You didn't say anything about it," Coley snapped quickly.

Joe's and Coley's eyes remained locked a moment.

"What's to say? Just that somebody asked about me."

Coley was frowning. "You got a couple of letters from Randolph, didn't you?"

"Yes. And from other schools, too. Okay?"

Coley waited a moment, and then nodded. "Okay," he said, still frowning.

Otherwise, there was no mention of Randolph all week—not from Coach Holliman and not from Joe's parents. The coach did not give Joe even a knowing glance or a questioning look. For Coach Holliman, it was business as usual preparing for the upcoming opponent. Joe's parents, he knew, were laying off to avoid distracting him in the face of the three remaining games.

Then Friday arrived.

"Let's go, let's go," Coach Holliman said, pacing around the parking lot alongside the school building. He had his clipboard in hand, checking off names as he waved the players onto the bus for the thirty-mile ride to Mount Holly.

Joe, Coley, Tracy, and Lew piled out of Tracy's van parked at the side of the lot and moved across toward the bus.

Moving through the crowd, Joe tried to match the excitement and enthusiasm of the players around him, but his jaw was clamped shut and his eyes stared straight ahead. He knew that the game had to squeeze out of his mind all thoughts of Randolph, Ryder State, open options, his friends' feelings—all of it. He'd been able to keep those thoughts at arm's length on the practice field all week. Now he had to do it during the game.

With an effort, he sang out, "Let's go-o-o!" and broke into a jog toward the bus.

# Chapter 6

◆     Standing at the side-line, watching Coley position himself at the fif-teen-yard line to receive the game's opening kickoff, Joe took a deep breath and exhaled. He stood without moving, his helmet dangling from his right hand.

Around him, some of the Hillcrest High play-ers were shouting encouragement to their team-mates on the field and cheering.

Down the sideline to Joe's left, Coach Holliman scowled at the scene on the field, looking for all the world like he had advance word of utter disaster.

The fans in the bleachers on both sides of the field were on their feet, waiting.

Joe glanced across the field at the crowd, mostly wearing green except for a knot of Hill-crest High fans in red at the forty-yard line. He wondered briefly if the crowd included a college scout there to watch the Hillcrest High quarter-back, Joe Mitchell, in action. Maybe so, he thought. The Randolph University Tigers had sent a scout from their campus in central Tennessee to watch him. Maybe tonight there was a scout from Kentucky. Or Iowa.

The Mount Holly kicker moved toward the ball, bringing Joe's mind back to the game at hand. The Mount Holly tacklers began their charge behind the kicker.

At the fifteen-yard line, Coley leaned forward slightly, arms hanging limply, watching. In front of him, the Hillcrest High blockers tensed.

The kicker sent the ball in a low end-over-end trajectory down the middle of the field.

Joe subconsciously took a step forward and watched Coley move up and take in the ball on the sixteen-yard line.

The low kick, with little hang time, gave Coley a chance to maneuver before the thundering crowd of Mount Holly tacklers reached him. He raced straight forward, up the middle of the field to the twenty-five-yard line, then cut to his right behind a devastating block by Lew and scampered down the sideline all the way to the forty-one-yard line before a tackler knocked him out of bounds. Coley scrambled back to his feet, laughing, in front of the Hillcrest High bench.

Joe pulled on his helmet and ran onto the

field. As he passed Coley coming off, they slapped hands.

Coley stepped back toward the bench to catch his breath for one play, and a substitute trotted onto the field to take his place in the backfield.

For Coach Holliman's Hillcrest High Cardinals, the first play from scrimmage was always the same: a simple handoff to Lew plunging into the middle of the line. "We want to test them where it counts," the coach liked to say.

Lew slammed into the line, fought his way through, bounced off a linebacker, and, legs churning, battled his way for eleven yards to a first down on the Mount Holly forty-eight-yard line.

The Cardinals had passed the opening test with flying colors.

Lew's plunge, following Coley's twenty-five-yard kickoff return, did not erase the frown from Coach Holliman's face, but Joe was grinning when he approached the huddle to call the second play from scrimmage.

Coley, reentering the game, raced to the huddle with a fist in the air in triumph.

Lew returned from the plunge with his usual blank expression. But his eyes revealed his excitement and he kept nodding his head as if saying the run was no accident.

Tracy shouted to Lew, "Hey, man!"

Joe nodded at Lew and said to everyone, "Let's go."

A pitchout to the right to Coley gained six yards. Then Tracy circled left end for seven yards and a first down on the Mount Holly thirty-five-yard line.

Joe, walking to the huddle, glanced at Coach Holliman at the sideline. The coach made no move, gave no signal. The call of the play was up to the quarterback on the field. Joe gave a slight nod of acknowledgment that, yes, the Cardinals were breaking on top, all was going well so far. When that was the case, Coach Holliman generally deferred to Joe's play-calling judgment. When the going was tough, though, the coach was constantly flashing signals from the sideline.

Joe leaned into the huddle. Time to test the Mount Holly defensive backs. Somebody from the Hillcrest Water Works had picked up the word that the Mount Holly secondary was pretty good. Well, let's see.

Joe called the play—a pass—and broke the huddle.

He took the snap and faked a handoff to Lew off tackle. Then, pulling the ball back in low and putting it on his hip, he rolled down the line to his right and began to drop back.

Tracy, breaking straight ahead, ran for ten yards. Then he cut sharply to his left, running across the field and going deeper, waggling his right hand in the air. A Mount Holly defensive back was with him.

Joe stopped, straightened, cocked his arm, and fired.

Tracy, stretching forward, took in the pass on the dead run, and the defensive back, a step behind, slammed into him immediately, bringing him down on the seventeen-yard line.

So much for the Mount Holly pass defense.

On the next play, Joe ran a quarterback option. When the Mount Holly defensive end committed himself to the elusive Coley moving out wide, Joe kept the ball and cut back inside behind the right tackle, Skip Matthews. Skip moved his man, giving Joe a hole. Joe dashed through, spun away from a linebacker, and faced only a defensive back between himself and the goal.

Joe ran straight for the last defender, who danced in place, waiting, ready to take the jolt head-on or to leap left or right. Joe looked right and lowered his right shoulder with a slight jerking motion. The tackler took the fake, and Joe cut back to his left and ran by the defender's frantic effort to reverse himself. The lunging defensive back got a hand on Joe, but nothing more. Joe ran into the end zone.

Joe circled in the end zone and tossed the

football to the referee, then ducked his head and jogged toward the huddle before the kick for the extra point.

Joe saw Lew and slapped hands with him. A grinning Coley gave Joe a hug. Tracy clapped Joe on the back.

Joe took it all with a smile, then stopped and looked around. He found the player he was seeking, and ran over to Skip Matthews. "Great block," he said. "That was your touchdown, not mine." Skip, who sometimes groused about the ball carriers getting all the glory, grinned back at him this time.

Harry Pearson was coming onto the field for the kick for the extra point and Coley was jogging toward the bench.

Joe watched Coley go. Then he saw Lew and Tracy moving toward the huddle. Suddenly, the whole drive for the touchdown flashed through his mind like a videotape rerun. Coley's kickoff return, and then his jitterbugging runs to the outside with a pitchout. Lew's powerful plunging. Tracy's running and pass receiving. Joe's own running and passing. They were, indeed, the backfield package.

Harry's kick, from Joe's hold, wobbled off to the left, no good, and the score stood at 6–0.

By halftime, the Cardinals led, 26–0.

Coach Holliman's scary assessment of the

Mount Holly Green Wave as a serious threat was barely a memory now to the grinning players in the dressing room during the intermission.

Coach Holliman, of course, looked like the Cardinals were trailing instead of leading by four touchdowns. Frown in place, he marched around the dressing room, from one player to another, offering advice here, criticism there, an occasional compliment, and always the warning: "This game isn't over yet."

When he came to Joe, he stared into his eyes a moment without speaking. Joe was so sure of the unspoken question—"You're going to be able to keep your mind on this game, aren't you, and keep all those other thoughts out of the way?"—that he almost answered, "I'm fine. I'm okay." But Joe didn't speak. He was happy to let his play in the first half speak for itself.

Coach Holliman finally nodded, as if he had asked his question and now was accepting Joe's reassurance. "Still the second half to play," he said.

Joe fought down an urge to grin at the solemn coach, the eternal pessimist. "Right," he said, keeping a straight face.

Through the second half, the thought of a college scout in the bleachers faded away and, as play followed play, Joe saw only the faces and figures of his friends in the backfield. The photograph of the jam-packed Randolph football stadium seemed very far away, and unclear.

The four of them were a machine, well-tuned through the years of playing together, functioning with perfection.

Joe handed off the ball to Lew plunging into the line with hardly a thought. He knew instinctively where to place the ball, and he knew that Lew was expecting the handoff in precisely that spot. And Lew took in the handoff smoothly and, legs pumping, slashed through the line.

Joe, trapped with the ball once when a defender broke through on Coley and made a pitchout impossible, turned and looked toward a run inside. That avenue was blocked. So he turned farther, knowing without a moment's doubt that Tracy, seeing Joe's dilemma, would somehow get himself free for a pass. And, sure enough, there was Tracy, loping into the open. Joe fired the ball across the field and Tracy caught it. A loss of yardage turned into a gain because Joe knew where Tracy would be, and Tracy knew Joe would be looking for him.

Going off tackle, needing only three yards for a first down, Joe ran into a wall of Mount Holly linemen charging shoulder to shoulder. He bounced off, turned, and of course there was Coley. Joe was not at all surprised to find his friend on the edge of the action, waiting in case he was needed. He flipped the ball in a lateral and Coley brought in the ball, whirled and ran to the outside of the defenders, gaining five yards and the needed first down.

How many times, Joe wondered, had he been saved by his friends in the backfield?

Lew, knowing exactly where Joe was going to put the handoff, made every one of Joe's hand-offs look like a masterpiece of smooth-flowing mechanics.

Tracy had good hands, sure, which helped any passer look good. But that wasn't what made the real difference. Tracy always seemed to know where Joe wanted to throw the ball, and he got himself to that place. A step slow, yes, but Tracy knew the passer who was throwing to him. Joe's passing looked all the better for it.

Coley, zigging this way and zagging that way, seemed always to be in the right place when Joe wanted to shovel the ball to the outside. Joe was a master of the pitchout—when it was Coley who was gathering it in.

As the scoreboard clock was winding down to the finish, with the Cardinals leading 54–7, Joe handed off one more time to Lew—smoothly, the timing perfect—and stepped back out of the way of the collision as Lew slammed into the line.

Joe wondered in that moment: What about handing off to a stranger plunging into the line? What about passing to a receiver who did not know Joe as Tracy did? How about pitchouts to a running back without Coley's innate ability to know where Joe wanted him to be?

The questions flew through Joe's mind, not needing to pause for an answer.

When the final seconds of the game ticked away and Joe and his teammates turned, shouting and cheering, for the run to the dressing room, the picture of Randolph University's giant stadium was nowhere in Joe's mind.

The dressing room was pandemonium.

Even Coach Holliman almost, but not quite, smiled as he moved among the shouting, cheering, laughing players.

The Mount Holly Green Wave was supposed to be tough, a team greatly improved since three early season losses. But the Cardinals buried them, 54–7.

Coley swung one arm around Joe's waist and raised the other arm in a gesture of triumph, shouting, "Wow! They couldn't stop us." The running back had scored two touchdowns, one on a sixty-yard punt return.

Joe grinned at his friend.

Coach Holliman walked by and said to Joe, "Good game." From Coach Holliman it was the ultimate compliment.

Joe had scored two more touchdowns after

the opening-drive sprint to the end zone, one on a five-yard keeper and the other on a twenty-two-yard run that started off right tackle. And he had passed for three touchdowns, two to Tracy and one to Benjy Moore, the Cardinals' tight end.

Joe grinned at Coach Holliman's compliment and said, "Thanks."

For a brief moment the color photograph of the Randolph University stadium flashed through his mind. He wished it hadn't. Then he saw in his mind the questioning expression on Coley's face when he'd asked Joe about Randolph, and he remembered the curious way Tracy and Lew waited silently for Joe's reply. Joe wished now that he hadn't ducked the question.

The coach watched Joe a moment, saying nothing.

Joe opened his mouth to speak, but now Coach Holliman was moving away, saying something to another player.

Joe had wanted to say that it was his friends—Coley grabbing pitchouts, Tracy catching passes, Lew taking handoffs into the line—that made him look good.

Later that night, in the basement den in Tracy's house, the four of them agreed the Cardinals were going to whip Marianna easily and defeat the tough Hoytville Cougars to win their second straight Rend Lake Conference championship.

And when Coley added that they were going to Ryder State next season and would win a championship, Joe said with a smile, "You bet."

## Chapter 7

The boys were halfway finished giving the van its regular Saturday morning wash job when Tracy's father came out the front door carrying his golf bag. He waved at the boys and walked across to the open garage door, stepped inside, opened the trunk of one of the two cars, dumped the clubs in, and slammed the trunk lid. He started walking around to the driver's side of the car, then stopped, turned, and approached the boys scrubbing the van.

"Joe," he said, "Harold Lanford was in the bank the other day, telling me that someone at Randolph University was expressing very real interest in you."

Joe turned from washing the rear window of the van and gave a little shrug and said, "Yeah, that's what Barbara was telling me."

The other three boys stopped washing to hear what Mr. Jackson was saying, and Joe noticed a frown on Tracy's face.

"Randolph is a great school," Mr. Jackson said. "And that's really bigtime college football, too, you know. I know you must be excited."

It was Joe's turn to frown. He was puzzled. Mr. Jackson knew as well as everyone else in Hillcrest about the boys' deal to stick together and go to Ryder State. But he gave no indication of it. He was acting as if there was no deal at all. In addition, nobody, and that included Mr. Jackson, knew about the second thoughts that had been rising up to plague Joe the past week. So what was going on here?

Joe mustered a smile and replied to Mr. Jackson, "I don't know. I doubt that it means anything. Just small talk, you know."

"That's not what Harold Lanford makes it sound like," Mr. Jackson said with a grin and a wave as he turned and walked back to his car.

For a moment, nobody said anything.

Then, as Mr. Jackson was backing out of the driveway, Joe and Coley spoke the same words at the same time to Tracy: "What was that all about?"

Lew was coming around from the side of the van to join them.

Joe suddenly recalled what his father had said at the kitchen table on Monday evening: "Willard Jackson may not want his son to attend Ryder State just so he can continue to play football with friends. . . . He may have plans that we don't know about."

Tracy's frown deepened.

"Doesn't he know about our deal?" Coley asked.

"Sure," Tracy said. "Sure he does."

"Then—?"

"I don't know," Tracy said. "Kind of weird." Then he added with a shrug, "But not to worry. I can handle my father when the time comes."

"C'mon, let's finish up and get moving," Joe said, silently agreeing that Tracy probably could handle his father—he always did—and besides he had heard enough of Randolph University the past week to last him a long time.

But on this Saturday there was no avoiding the subject of someone at Randolph University expressing interest in Joe Mitchell. The Hillcrest grapevine, while slow in picking up on the report, now was in full swing. The fact was obvious at every turn in the boys' day.

Barely minutes out of the Jackson driveway, when Tracy pulled into Jimmy West's gasoline station for a fill-up, the question popped up again.

Jimmy West, who had played end for the Cardinals about ten years earlier and remained an avid fan, left the cashier's cage while Tracy was pumping the gas and walked across to the window of the van. "You going to take up Randolph on that offer, Joe, instead of the four of you sticking together at Ryder State?" he asked.

Joe shook his head. "There's no offer. Just somebody mentioned my name. That's all."

Jimmy grinned at Joe. "That's not the way I heard it," he said.

When Tracy had finished filling the tank and paid for the gas and they were moving out of the station, Joe said to no one in particular, "Good grief!"

None of the others commented.

Then, at Ellie's Cafe, Ellie herself, peering over the cash register when the boys entered, said to Joe: "You go on down there and play for Randolph. That's bigtime, and you're bigtime." Joe smiled at her and kept walking. Ellie wasn't one to ask questions. She dealt in advice.

Joe turned and said to Coley, "Well, it's a free country."

Coley said, "Umm."

Barbara Lanford entered with a couple of other girls. She gave Joe a little wave as they took seats in a booth across the cafe. Joe waved back and smiled at her. It was one week ago that she had started to tell him what happened at Randolph. It was six days ago that she did tell him. What if she and her parents had not visited Randolph? What if the word of Randolph's interest had never gotten back to Joe? He would have spent the week happily preparing for the Mount Holly game and planning on going to Ryder State with his friends. Or would Coach Holliman have said something? No, for sure not. The coach said he had wanted to wait until the season was over. Well, the Lanfords' story was out now, and Joe had heard it, and everyone had heard it.

Shortly before noon, the four of them arrived at Happy Andy's on the highway for hamburgers for lunch. Coley was due for work at the Wiggams' Drug Store soda fountain at one o'clock, and Lew was scheduled to join his father on a construction job at about the same time. They had an hour before parting, planning to regroup in the evening for the Rotary Club's Harvest Moon barbecue.

Happy Andy also had advice.

"Don't listen to any of that talk from those big and fancy schools, Joe," he said. "You boys stick together. You're a team."

Coley, across from Joe, and the others watched without speaking while Joe nodded and smiled at Happy Andy and said, "Right. Sure. You bet, Andy."

In the afternoon, Joe and his father cut the grass, front and back, although the lawn barely needed the cutting. The growing season was nearing an end. Surely this was the last cutting of the year.

At the finish the two of them sat on the edge of the wooden deck off the back of the house, each with a can of soft drink.

"We haven't talked—not really, that is—since you spoke with Coach Holliman," his father said. "Your mother and I knew you were concentrating on the Mount Holly game." He paused. "But I guess you've had some time to do some thinking about what you want to do."

"Everybody in town seems to have an opinion," Joe said.

"Yes. Everyone at the Water Works was asking me about it this morning. The word is all over town."

They sat for a moment without speaking, and then Joe said, "I think the best thing for me is to go to Ryder State with the guys. They're my friends, and . . . " He finished the sentence with a shrug instead of words.

"That's the way it looks to you right now, huh?"

Joe looked at his father. The words "right now" seemed to have been spoken with added emphasis. "Yeah," he said finally.

"Things may change, and you should—"

"I know," Joe said with a laugh, "I'll keep my options open."

"Well, yes," his father said.

Then Joe, remembering Mr. Jackson's puzzling manner, said, "Sure."

Then, on Sunday morning, the *St. Louis Journal-Gazette* appeared with its story about the college football prospects in the area high schools.

To Joe, the story at first was exciting. There he was, listed as one of the three best quarterback prospects in the *Journal-Gazette*'s circulation area of southern Illinois, eastern Missouri, and western Kentucky. The area represented a lot of high schools, all with quarterbacks, and there was Joe—ranked in the top three.

A line drawing of Joe's face and the other two quarterbacks stared out at him from the page. The sketch of Joe resembled the photograph the *Hillcrest Light* had published with its preseason story on the Cardinals. The *Journal-Gazette* must have obtained a print from the *Light* and had an artist copy it. Joe was flattered that the big-city newspaper went to so much trouble to display a likeness of him.

He began reading about himself.

Joe Mitchell was, the story said, strong, smart, and talented. He was "a coach on the field," a quarterback whose coach allowed him to call a lot of the plays on his own. He was a team leader. He was a good runner. He had the potential to become a great passer.

Well, okay.

Then he read on, and began to frown. According to the article, he "single-handedly lifted the Hillcrest High Cardinals to the Rend Lake Conference championship last year" and was in the process of doing it again this year.

Oh? Single-handedly? His frown deepened.

There was more.

Joe had, the story said, racked up "remarkable achievements without having the benefit of teammates of equal caliber." Naming no names, the story said that Joe's favorite receiver was slow and his running back was "quick but too small to be consistently effective." And, the story went on, "Mitchell operates behind a line that is short on both strength and skill." Joe flinched as he thought of Skip Matthews, Charlie Garrison, and the others in the forward wall.

The writer asked the question, "How good a quarterback might Joe Mitchell be with fast receivers and strong runners capable of sharing the load and a line able to protect him?"

And then: "At tiny Hillcrest High, with its one-man coaching staff, Mitchell's progress has been largely self-propelled. He's due a quick quantum leap in ability under adequate tutelage." The slap at Coach Holliman sent a blush across Joe's face.

Joe looked up from the paper.

His father was seated across the table, reading the main news section of the *Journal-Gazette*.

His mother was clearing away the last of the breakfast dishes.

All three were dressed to leave shortly for church services.

"Good grief!" Joe blurted.

He felt a wild desire to race around Hillcrest, knocking on the door of each house and taking their copy of the *Journal-Gazette* sports section away from them.

"Uh-huh," his father said with a nod, lowering his section of the paper to the table.

"You read all this?"

His father frowned. "Yes," he said. "It's pretty brutal. But there's nothing you can do about it. You didn't say those things. The sportswriter did. It's not your fault. Don't let it worry you. Besides, there is nothing you can do about it."

"Yes, there is," Joe said. "I've got to call Tracy and Coley—and Coach Holliman—and, jeez, all the guys in the line." He shook his head slightly. "This is terrible."

"After church," his father said, getting to his feet.

"Church? I can't show up there—"

"Joe, everyone will know that you didn't write it—didn't say those things about the others. So just, well, nod and smile and shrug your shoulders."

And that is what Joe did. He listened to the comments, forced a smile, and shrugged.

But he did not smile while he sat in the church, and he did not hear a single word of the service. The story would have been bad enough at any time. But right now—on the heels of the Lanfords' story about Randolph University, when the whole town was asking if Joe was going to stick with the backfield package, or pull out and go his own way alone. First, Joe Mitchell was good enough to play for Randolph—too good to stick with his friends. That was bad enough. And now this. He almost shivered at the thought of what Coley was going to have to say. And Tracy. And Lew. Not to mention Skip Matthews, Charlie Garrison, and the others in the line.

Back home, the church service finally having ended, Joe seated himself at the telephone and began dialing.

Coley, speaking in a flat tone, said, "Well, maybe it's all true."

Joe paused a moment, more concerned by Coley's tone than his words. Then he said, "Nah, what does that sportswriter know? I'll bet he never even saw us play."

"Maybe," Coley said. Then he added, "Do you suppose Coach Holliman said those things about us—the rest of us, I mean—to the sportswriter?"

The statement had a chilling effect on Joe. If all the players got the idea that Coach Holliman had blown up Joe into a superhero and put down everyone else, the result could be disastrous.

"Of course not," Joe almost shouted. "The writer made a pretty mean crack about Coach Holliman, too, you know. Didn't you see that?"

"Yeah," Coley said. "I was just wondering."

"Well, don't wonder."

Tracy seemed embarrassed when he came to the telephone to take Joe's call. "Well, now the whole world knows that I'm a step slow," he said in a feeble effort at making a joke.

"I thought the whole story was horrible, and wrong," Joe said.

"It doesn't matter," Tracy said.

"That's right," Joe said, with all the forcefulness he could muster. "It doesn't matter."

Joe began to dial Lew's number. Then he stopped. At Lew's house, they did not receive the *St. Louis Journal-Gazette*. Probably Lew did not even know about the story, unless Coley or Tracy had called him. Either way, Lew would not have read it.

He considered calling Charlie Garrison and maybe Skip Matthews and some of the others in the line. But what was there to say? Almost anything would sound silly, if not, to use a word his mother called up occasionally, patronizing.

Joe sat a moment, hand still on the receiver, staring at the wall. Then he picked up the telephone directory, looked up Coach Holliman's home number, and dialed.

The coach's first statement was, "I told you last week not to believe anything in the story, didn't I?"

Joe nodded into the telephone, not speaking for a moment. Then he said, "But—"

"But, what?"

Joe took a deep breath and plunged ahead. "Did you say all those things about us? I mean, about Tracy and Coley and the guys in the line?"

"No, I didn't. The sportswriter didn't even ask about anyone else on the team. I suspect he called the coaches of a couple of teams on our schedule, and that's what they told him." He gave a small laugh and added, "I didn't say those bad things about myself, either."

"Okay."

"It'll blow over," Coach Holliman said.

Joe hoped so.

He wound up passing the afternoon with his father, watching the Chicago Bears defeat the Philadelphia Eagles, and wondering if the *St. Louis Journal-Gazette* sportswriter might have had it right.

# Chapter 8

◆        Joe and Coley and Lew were standing together in the milling throng of students gathered in the lobby before the bell signaling the first class of the day. Lew had been filled in on the *Journal-Gazette* story the day before by both Coley and Tracy, so Joe was spared a detailed recapitulation. He still faced, though, the comments and questioning looks from the students moving around in the lobby in the last minutes before the first bell.

To Joe's relief, most of the remarks were more wisecrack than anything else, making an easy response a simple matter.

"Hey, superhero," somebody said.

"Yeah," Joe replied with a grin.

Another expressed mock astonishment at seeing Joe in the lobby and said, "I thought by now you'd be on your way to join the Chicago Bears."

"They're sending a plane for me this afternoon," Joe said.

Oddly, the toughest to answer was a serious-faced student, peering intently into Joe's eyes, who said simply, "I read about you in the *Journal-Gazette*."

What's to say? Joe finally replied, "Oh, did you?"

Coley looked uneasy during the exchanges, as if fearing someone would make a crack about the running back being "too small to be consistently effective." But nobody did.

The most uncomfortable moment for Joe did not involve a remark. It involved silence. Skip Matthews, frowning, walked past him without speaking. He was past Joe, and moving on, before Joe realized what had happened. He started to call out to Skip and go after him.

But at that moment Tracy, with an expression of alarm on his face, came moving through the crowd toward them. He reached them and stopped, seeming breathless.

"What's wrong?" Joe asked.

"Man!" Tracy blurted.

"What?" Coley asked.

Tracy took a deep breath, glanced around, and then spoke in a lowered voice. "Well, it's not good news."

The other three waited.

"My father told me this morning that he's got

me lined up to visit a bunch of college campuses that he's picked out—'suitable colleges,' he said—starting right after the end of football season."

None of the other three spoke. Coley frowned. Joe pursed his lips slightly, as if uttering a soundless, "Oh?" He remembered Mr. Jackson's curious remarks of Saturday morning, speaking to Joe as if the boys never had had a plan to stick together. Lew glanced from Tracy to Joe.

The wide-eyed Tracy looked at his three friends and said, "And Ryder State is not on his list."

This time, Joe said it aloud, "Oh?"

"Yes—oh," Tracy said.

Lew, who usually let the other three do the talking, said, "Does this mean . . . " and then let the sentence trail off.

"What?" Coley said sharply. "Doesn't he know?"

"Doesn't he know?" Tracy repeated. "Sure he knows. I've told him plenty of times."

"Well, then—"

"Wait a minute," Joe said, waving Coley into silence. He glanced up at the lobby clock. A little over five minutes before the bell. He turned back to Tracy. "What did your father say when you told him that we've decided we want to go to the same school? What did he say when you talked about Ryder State?"

Tracy gave Joe a blank stare. So accustomed to always getting what he wanted, Tracy was clearly taken aback by even a hint of a suggestion that his father, or anyone, would have an objection to his plans. Finally, he said, "Well, nothing." Tracy paused, as if trying to remember some words of his father's. "No, nothing, really. Usually, 'We'll see,' or something like that. But he's never said anything for or against. Until this morning."

Tracy's recounting of his father's reactions rang a familiar bell in Joe's mind. The response sounded exactly like what he had been hearing from his own parents. Then Joe recalled his father's remark that Mr. Jackson might have other plans for Tracy, and wondered if Tracy's father had said that Joe Mitchell might have other plans than Ryder State.

Out of the corner of his eye, Joe caught Coley watching him—Joe—and not Tracy while Tracy explained his father's previously noncommittal attitude. Joe was sure that Coley was having the same thought that was now racing through Joe's mind. If Tracy pulled out, there was no backfield package, and Joe was off the hook. He was free to look around on his own. He was free to consider Randolph University.

Joe brought himself back to the present and focused on Tracy. "Exactly what happened?" he asked. "What did he say?"

"Just what I said. We were having breakfast, everything perfectly normal, you know, when all of a sudden, like he was talking about the weather or something, he announced that he had written to these schools, and that we would be making all these visits, and then we'd be making a decision."

Coley leaned in. He was looking at Tracy now. "What did you say to him when he said this?"

"Say to him? What could I say? I didn't have time to say anything. He brought this up at breakfast, just before I had to leave. There wasn't any time to explain anything." He paused. Then, as if the thought only now occurred for the first time, he said, "I'll bet that's why he said it at breakfast. He knew there wouldn't be time for me to argue with him."

Joe gave a tight little smile at the suggestion. "Yeah, probably," he said.

The bell rang, hailing the students to their first class of the day. The four of them turned together and walked out of the lobby toward the corridor.

"Well, I'll be home tonight, and there won't be any hurry then," Tracy said. "I'll have time to argue tonight."

"Right," Coley said as he parted from them to enter a classroom.

Tracy headed in another direction, and then Lew.

Joe, walking alone the last steps toward Mrs. Henderson's study hall, did not know whether to feel concern or relief. On Friday night, in the exhilaration of the game, he had found it easy to decide that he wanted to stick with his friends in the backfield package. Then on Saturday he found himself, well, sometimes less certain. But he had, in the end, told his father of his decision to go to Ryder State with his friends. Then on Sunday he had to admit to himself that he could not help wondering about the decision after reading the story in the *St. Louis Journal-Gazette*. Now it appeared Mr. Jackson had created a problem, or solved one.

Joe took a breath and said to himself, "At least it saved us from having to talk about the *St. Louis Journal-Gazette* story."

Then somebody passing by said, "Hey, Joe, how's it feel to be great?"

Joe gave a small wave and a grin, and entered the study hall. He was still going to hear about that story for a while.

And Joe did hear more about the newspaper story as he moved through the day, occasionally needing more than a smile and a shrug to reply.

"Did you speak to the sports reporter who wrote that story in the *Journal-Gazette*?" asked Mr. Crain, a history teacher who had been around Hillcrest High almost as long as Coach Holliman.

Joe frowned at the unexpected question, then said, "No, I didn't."

"I'm glad to hear that," Mr. Crain said. "Some of it was very unflattering to Hillcrest High, Coach Holliman, and your teammates."

Joe's frown deepened.

Barbara Lanford met Joe in the corridor with a wide smile and one word: "Wow!"

Joe shook his head and grinned.

"I've been telling everyone all morning that you might be a superstar famous quarterback, but I beat you in tennis a week ago," Barbara said.

Joe gave a laugh, as Barbara was expecting, and then walked on, his smile fading away. He did not enjoy the reminder that the tennis date was when it all started—his world going crazy, no longer the comfortable life of his friends and himself having the fun of winning games and looking ahead to Ryder State together.

At noon in the cafeteria, a student walked by the table where Joe and the others were eating, grinned, and said, "Well, it's slow-foot and little-bit and the star."

Coley had been explaining to Tracy and the others that Tracy always got what he wanted, and would get Ryder State if that was what he wanted, and so there was nothing to worry about. Joe looked up at the interruption and watched the student walk on without waiting for a response. Then he looked at Coley, Tracy, and Lew. They all were watching him.

"Look," Joe said, "I didn't write the story. I didn't even talk to the reporter. It's not my fault."

Nobody spoke.

Then Coley said, "We all know that."

But not everyone was accepting so easily the newspaper's elevation of Joe to stardom and the implied putdown of the other players and even the coach.

Charlie Garrison, Joe's partner on almost every snap from center the last three years, caught up with him in the corridor heading to the last class of the day. "About that story in the *Journal-Gazette*," Charlie said.

Charlie usually wore a happy expression, always ready to smile. But he turned a somber face to Joe.

Joe sighed. "Yeah, what about it?" he said, with more than a touch of weariness and exasperation in his voice. He had taken all of it, the jokes, the needles, the unpleasant suggestion of Mr. Crain, even the stares of Coley, Tracy, and Lew.

"Well, it's just that—well, it didn't set well with some of the guys."

Joe looked at Charlie. He recalled Skip Matthews pointedly walking past him without speaking in the lobby before the first class. But all he said was, "It didn't set well with me, either, but there's nothing I can do about it."

Charlie nodded, apparently satisfied with Joe's answer. Then he returned to being Charlie Garrison—gave a smile—and said, "You know how it is with us guys in the line."

Joe suddenly was very weary of the whole subject, tired of fielding wisecracks. "No," he said with a touch of sarcasm in his voice, "I don't know. How is it with you guys in the line?"

Charlie's smile faded as quickly as it had appeared, and Joe regretted snapping at him.

"I'm sorry," Joe said. "It's just that I've been hearing about that darned story all day long."

Charlie nodded. "I just thought that it's best that you know."

"Know what?"

Charlie gave a little shrug. "Well, if that story had been about me—you know?—well, if it'd been about me, I might be having trouble with a big head."

"Do you think I've got a big head?"

"No."

"But some of the others on the team—some of the guys in the line—may be thinking so."

"Yeah, maybe," Charlie said.

"Okay, and thanks for telling me."

Joe turned into the classroom for his last class before going down to dress for practice.

Joe felt the coolness when he walked into the dressing room.

The remarks aimed at Joe all through the day might well have added up to a strong clue to the thinking of his teammates. But they didn't. He had responded to the comments—the funny and the irritating and the troublesome—one at a time, without seeing a pattern.

Even Charlie's warning was, well, only about getting a big head, and Joe had no worries about that.

But a lot of the faces now turned toward him as he walked to his locker told the story. His teammates might not blame Joe for the story. Maybe they did not even think he was getting a big head. But nonetheless they resented the story. And Joe, blameless or not, was the cause of the resentment.

## Chapter 9

◆ The practice session beginning the longest week in Joe's life was glum, very glum. There was no life to it.

Among the offensive linemen, and even among some of the players on the defense, there were a lot of glacial stares and surly glaring aimed at Joe.

While his friends seemed to have accepted the fact that the newspaper story was not Joe's fault, they now faced the threat of Tracy being pulled out of the backfield package.

Tracy went through the motions of the light Monday signal drill. But clearly he remained every bit as stunned as he had appeared that morning in the lobby. The number of dropped passes revealed his lack of concentration. His mind was on other things.

Coley, always laughing and chattering, always enjoying practice as much as any game, was silent and frowning. The word from Tracy's father served only to add to his nagging doubts about Joe. The joy in his skittering style of running was missing. His thoughts were elsewhere.

Lew seldom showed emotion, whether on the practice field or in the closing moments of a tight game. So the change in mood showed less in him. But Lew knew of Coley's suspicions about Joe, and he knew what Tracy's father had said. Joe knew Lew well enough to read the concern in his mind.

As for Joe, he watched his preoccupied friends in the backfield and saw the unfriendly expressions on the faces of many of the other players, and he found it increasingly difficult to keep up the shouts of encouragement, the cheers that pulled a team of individuals together.

Watching Tracy absently take his eye off the ball and miss a pass, Joe wondered how Tracy's father possibly could have made his disturbing announcement at this particular time. Mr. Jackson knew as well as anyone that the Cardinals were two important victories away from the Rend Lake Conference championship. Wouldn't he know enough to realize the damage he was doing?

Coach Holliman's raspy shout interrupted Joe's thoughts. "Mitchell, come back to the practice, will you?"

Joe gave a sharp nod of the head and turned back to the business at hand. With a twinge of guilt, he realized he was letting his concentration waver as much as the rest of them.

"He was just thinking about how good he is," mumbled one of the players.

Joe looked around at the player, Skip Matthews, who turned away. Joe said nothing.

Then Charlie Garrison said, "Cut it out."

Joe still said nothing, but glanced across at Coach Holliman. Had the coach heard the remark? Joe couldn't tell. The coach was moving toward another player.

Joe took the snap for the next play and flipped the ball out to Coley running wide to the right. Then, standing back while Coley ran out the play, Joe could not help letting his mind wander again.

Did Coach Holliman know what was going on with Tracy and the other players?

Joe found himself simply assuming that the coach knew about Tracy's father threatening to break up the plans of the backfield package. Coach Holliman always seemed to know everything. Perhaps Mr. Jackson had told the coach of his plans.

But, if so, why hadn't the coach said something to them, or at least said something to Tracy to put his mind back on track, concentrating on the game ahead?

For sure, Coach Holliman knew that at least some members of the team were concerned about the story in the *St. Louis Journal-Gazette*. Joe himself had told the coach as much.

That being the case, Joe had endured the coolness in the dressing room, thinking that Coach Holliman surely would open practice with a talk to the team. He would tell the players that neither he nor Joe was responsible for the words the sportswriter had written, and that everyone should promptly forget it.

But the coach sent the players onto the field without a word, divided up the assignments as he normally did, and set the players to work without a single reference to the story.

Maybe he was refusing to dignify the story with a comment. Or maybe he was insisting, as he sometimes did, that his players were mature enough to handle the situation without being lectured to as if they were kindergarten kids.

Whatever the reason, Joe was puzzled and troubled by the coach's silence.

Maybe, Joe thought with a frown, Coach Holliman didn't recognize the depth of the feeling among some of the players.

"Mitchell, wake up and play football," Coach Holliman barked.

"Right," Joe said.

Finally, the light signal-drill practice came to an end. And, finally, Joe had showered and dressed, and he, Coley, Tracy, and Lew were walking away from the school, headed for home in the darkening evening.

"I'll get this business straightened out to-night," Tracy announced without preamble.

Joe glanced at Tracy. The suddenness of the statement seemed good evidence that the matter had been on Tracy's mind all day, probably through all of his classes and certainly through-out football practice.

"Uh-huh," Coley said, sounding not certain at all.

"Look," Joe said, "don't get in a fight with him about it. Not right now. We've got a couple of games to concentrate on. You can get in a battle with him later."

Almost angrily, Tracy turned to Joe, thrust his jaw out, and said, "I want it settled, and right now."

But Tracy did not get the matter settled.

"All I could get out of him was, 'We'll see,' " Tracy told Joe in a telephone call shortly before Joe went to bed.

Judging by the lateness of the hour, Joe could imagine a very long and heated discussion. "Don't worry about it right now," Joe said. "Like I told you, we've got two games to win. Plenty of time to hash it out after we've won the cham-pionship."

"That's what Coley said, too."

"He's right."

"He said one funny thing, though."

"Who? Coley?"

"No. My father. He said that when he read the *Journal-Gazette* story about you and remembered the story out of Randolph, he realized that you weren't going to go to Ryder State anyway, and that's why he went ahead and told me about his list of colleges for me to visit."

Joe was silent a moment.

In that moment, Tracy said, "Is that right?"

Joe stalled. "Is what right?"

"That you're not going to Ryder State."

Joe took a deep breath. He remembered his decision of Friday night. He was going to stick with his friends, keep the backfield intact. But then one of them had a father saying it wasn't going to happen. And when that happened, Joe found himself—to his surprise—more relieved than troubled. Joe finally said, "Tracy, it's not me who is saying no and it's not my father who is saying no. It's your father who is saying no."

It was Tracy's turn to be silent a moment.

Joe continued, "None of us knows what's going to happen. But the immediate problem is beating Marianna and then Hoytville." He paused. "Then we'll see what happens—and we'll see what your father says."

Tracy was silent again for a moment, and then said, "Yeah."

Practice got no better, and Joe found himself thanking his lucky stars that the upcoming opponent was the lackluster Marianna Panthers and not the powerhouse Hoytville Cougars. The Panthers had lost four games in their dismal season. They were no match for the Cardinals, even a troubled Cardinals team.

Because the Panthers offered only the mildest of threats, Coach Holliman was introducing no new plays, no tricks, no innovations in the Cardinals' attack. There was nothing new to learn, nothing new to master in the four days of drills leading up to the game on Friday night. Coach Holliman clearly wanted to defeat the Marianna Panthers without showing a scout from Hoytville High anything new. He was saving any surprises for the dangerous Cougars.

So Joe and the other players were able to slog their way through the drills with their minds elsewhere, suffering only the occasional bark from the coach.

Joe thought on Tuesday, and then again on Wednesday, that surely the backfield's preoccupation with Tracy's father and the other players' reactions to the *Journal-Gazette* story would fade away and the Cardinals would come back to life. But it didn't happen.

Walking home on Wednesday evening, Joe said to his friends, "We're flat, you know. Really flat."

"It's only Marianna," Tracy said matter-of-factly.

"We'll beat them," Coley said.

"No, I'm worried," Joe said. "It's not just you or me. It's almost everyone."

"Nothing to worry about," Coley said. "Once the game starts, everyone will be okay. You'll see."

"Sometimes a good team gets upset," Joe said. "When they're overconfident, or just plain not ready."

"Not to worry," Coley said.

But it was obvious the next day, Thursday, that Coach Holliman was worried. In an unusual move for the day before a game, he sent the Cardinals through a lengthy full-speed scrimmage.

The racing and bumping and tackling, nonstop for almost two hours, was a time-proven antidote for wandering minds. The player who wasn't alert got knocked down. He got hit by a blow he hadn't seen coming. He misstepped into a collision he did not want.

The antidote worked, and quickly.

Joe found the full-speed contact invigorating—fighting his way through the line, breaking tackles, dodging the charging linemen to get a pass away.

Tracy's indifferent stare vanished with the first sound of a running tackler determined to slam him to the ground. Tracy kept his eyes on the ball. He ducked and looped and weaved to break free for Joe's passes.

Coley, facing the prospect of bone-rattling tackles, put his mind to the serious business of eluding tacklers. He spun and wriggled and ran his way to big gains.

Lew looked no different. He slammed into the line with power. He laid tacklers low with devastating blocks.

The linemen on either side of Charlie's center position worked hard. They had no time for grumbling and grousing about the quarterback being the star of a story in the *St. Louis Journal-Gazette*. They struggled to make their blocks.

At the finish, weary and dirty and sweaty, Joe stood in the shower and enjoyed the needles of hot water. He felt good.

And then he wondered: Was one good day of practice enough, even for the hapless Marianna Panthers?

The pep rally was over.

At the rear of the auditorium, the students

were streaming out the doors into the lobby, heading for their lockers to pick up jackets and books and head for home.

On the stage at the front of the auditorium, Joe moved into the single-file line of players heading down the six steps at the side.

Coach Holliman had given the Hillcrest High students his usual frown and the standard doom-laden speech about how tough the game was going to be, ending with the familiar advice that their cheers from the bleachers were worth points on the field.

Now walking up the aisle, Joe looked at the familiar scene—the students moving out, the players walking in a line, the smudged cream-colored walls, the empty seats—and thought that the last pep rally seemed like it was a year ago, rather than a week. How long ago did the Cardinals defeat Mount Holly and Joe decide, finally and absolutely, to stick with the backfield package? Only a week?

Joe stopped by his locker, then joined Coley and Lew in the lobby to await Tracy's arrival, and then the four of them began the walk home.

For Joe, the next two hours at home—from the end of the pep rally to his arrival back at school to dress out for the game—was the longest period of the week during football season.

His mother always had a sandwich and a glass of milk ready for him because there was no

heavy dinner before a game. As always, he daw-
dled over the meal at the kitchen table to kill
time. Then he glanced at the *Hillcrest Light*. Finally, his father arrived home. And a few minutes later, at last, he heard the honking of
Tracy's van out front. It was time to go.

Joe never had been troubled by pregame nervousness. Some of his teammates, he knew, suffered terrible cases of the jitters. But for Joe, the
two hours before a game was a time of anticipa-
tion. He was eager to get on with playing the
game.

But on this day, as he grabbed his jacket and
headed out the door, he was nervous.

## Chapter 10

◆ Joe's feeling of nervousness would not go away. Not during the ride to the school. Not while he was changing into his pads and uniform. Not during the warm-up drills. Not during the coin toss.

And not now, as he stood at the sideline watching Harry Pearson place the ball down for the game's opening kickoff.

He kept taking deep breaths, but they didn't help.

It was strange, really strange.

Then he knew what was causing it.

Unpreparedness equaled nervousness. Joe had seen it happen in the classroom. Going into a test without full preparation, he was nervous. But when well prepared, he was not. He had noticed this as early as the ninth grade, and decided that preparation was preferable to nervousness, not to mention a bad grade. He was never nervous before a football game because he was well prepared. Until tonight.

None of them were well-prepared, following the sluggish practice week.

Tracy, not concentrating, had dropped passes in practice. Was he going to be concentrating tonight, or dropping passes? Coley was flat in practice, until he finally came alive in the Thursday scrimmage. Which was he going to be tonight? Lew, although undoubtedly distracted himself, always was tough, unvarying in his performance. But Lew could not do it all.

Neither could Joe Mitchell—a nervous Joe Mitchell.

Joe recalled the grumbles and scowls of the linemen during the week. Their practice week had not been a good one. If the blockers gave less than their best, the quarterback didn't have a chance. And even if the blockers did give their best, a quarterback lacking confidence in his blockers was sure to sputter and stall. Were the blockers prepared to give their best? Joe did not know.

Joe looked around. To his right, Tracy stood, his helmet dangling from his right hand, staring out onto the field. His expression was serious, determined. Maybe that was good. But Tracy usually was all grins just before a game.

At Joe's left, Coley and Lew stood together. Coley, usually electric with excitement at the moment of the opening kickoff, looked like his mind was a million miles away. Well, he was able to sparkle during the Thursday scrimmage. Maybe he would do it tonight when the time came to play. Lew, as always, wore a blank expression.

None of it helped Joe's feeling of nervousness.

Joe recalled Tracy's response to Joe's concern about the Cardinals being flat: "It's only Marianna." And Coley had added, "We'll beat them."

Well, maybe, Joe thought, and took another deep breath.

On the field, Harry backed up and waited. At the referee's signal, he moved forward for the kickoff.

The bleachers on both sides of the field were filled to capacity, the fans on their feet for the opening play.

Harry kicked the ball high and short and a little to the left.

The Marianna receiver plunged forward and veered sharply to bring himself under the falling ball. He juggled the ball momentarily while running. Then he got a grip on it with both hands and let his momentum carry him forward and toward the far sideline. He got a good block at the thirty-yard line and raced to the thirty-seven before a couple of Hillcrest High tacklers bounced him out of bounds.

Joe stepped back and tried another deep breath as the Cardinals' defense moved onto the field for the Marianna Panthers' first play from scrimmage.

Coach Holliman paced the sideline, then came to a stop next to Joe. They stood together and watched as the Marianna fullback hit the middle of the line, gaining three yards.

"If we get the ball back on the good side of the forty, pass on first down," Coach Holliman said.

Joe nodded. He thought he understood Coach Holliman's strategy. The Hillcrest High Cardinals always hit the middle on the first play, a plunge by fullback Lew Preston. The Hoytville Cougars surely knew this. So an uncharacteristic pass on first down, for the benefit of the Hoytville High scout who certainly was in the bleachers tonight, might pay off a week later. And, of course, it might pay off right now, surprising the Marianna Panthers. But clearly Hoytville was in the coach's mind.

Coach Holliman promptly marched away, pacing down the sideline, his face turned to the play on the field. The Marianna quarterback did a poor job of faking a pass, and pitched out to a runner heading around right end. The play fooled nobody and a swarm of Hillcrest High tacklers smothered the runner at the line of scrimmage for no gain. Third down and seven yards to go on the Marianna High forty-yard line.

Joe looked over to Tracy. "You heard?"

"Yeah." But still no smile, just grim determination.

The Marianna quarterback tried a pass and
failed, overthrowing his receiver. It was fourth
down and seven yards to go, and both kicking
teams jogged onto the field.

"Go, Coley!" Joe shouted, although he didn't
feel like it.

Watching his friend position himself to receive the punt, Joe had a horrible premonition
that Coley, who never fumbled, was going to
fumble. The ball was going to bounce all the way
to the end zone, where one of the Panthers was
going to cover it for a touchdown, and the
Cardinals were going to be trailing before they
ran their first play.

But Coley didn't fumble. He took in the punt
on the Hillcrest High twenty-eight-yard line,
tucked the ball away, and raced toward the near
sideline. He passed the thirty, then the thirty-
five, and spun away from a tackler before going
down on the forty-two-yard line.

That, as Coach Holliman had put it, was the
"good side of the forty."

Joe pulled on his helmet and led the offense
unit onto the field. Coley had not fumbled the
punt. He had run it back fourteen yards. As for
Tracy, maybe an expression of grim determination was not all bad. Joe glanced at the linemen
running onto the field with him. He saw nothing

that told him anything. Their expressions looked the same as always.

Everything was going to be all right, Joe told himself as he jogged toward Charlie Garrison setting up the huddle.

Joe leaned into the huddle and called the play—a pass to Tracy cutting toward the left sideline.

Lining up behind Charlie, Joe scanned the Marianna defense. The Panthers had done their homework, for sure. They knew, as well as everyone else, that Coach Holliman's Cardinals sent the fullback into the center of the line on their first play from scrimmage. So, there they were, linemen shoulder to shoulder, linebackers up close and eyeing the middle of the line, and even the defensive backs taking up positions a couple of steps forward.

Without his nervousness, without the picture in his mind of Tracy's frozen expression, Joe would have viewed the scene in front of him as sure touchdown material. An unexpected pass to Tracy cutting to the left sideline, a defensive back out of position and off-balance—and Tracy running to the goal untouched. But Joe, as he took the snap, did feel the nervousness and did see Tracy's unsmiling face in his mind.

Joe stepped back with the ball, turned, and extended it to Lew plunging into the center of the line. At the last second, he withdrew the ball. Lew hit the line empty-handed, drawing the instant attention of everyone in the Marianna defense.

The ball on his hip, Joe rolled back to his right and looked for Tracy.

He was out there, ten yards deep, making his cut toward the sideline, only now catching the eye of the Marianna defensive back.

Tracy looked back at Joe as he ran. The defensive back, certain now of the danger, was in pursuit.

Joe brought up his arm, cocked, and fired.

Tracy, galloping safely ahead of the frantic defensive back, extended both hands and caught the ball without breaking stride.

The fans in the bleachers on both sides of the field leaped to their feet with a giant roar as Tracy pulled in the ball and turned toward the goal, forty-five yards away, with nothing but space in front of him.

Joe danced in place a half-dozen yards behind the line of scrimmage, shooting both fists in the air, more in relief than exultation.

And then, in the blink of an eye, Tracy and the ball parted company.

There was Tracy, running, and there was the ball, floating in the air away from him, to his right.

The crowd suddenly fell silent, then let out a long, low "Ooooh."

Joe blinked, his fists still in the air. He brought his arms down.

Tracy slammed on the brakes and, turning sharply, made a frantic dive for the drifting ball. But he tripped over his own feet in turning and crashed to the ground short of the ball.

The Marianna defensive back coming up behind Tracy fell on the ball for a fumble recovery.

Joe stared in disbelief. A sure touchdown had, in a split second, changed into a lost fumble. It was Marianna's ball on the Panthers' forty-two-yard line. Joe pulled off his helmet and walked toward the sideline as the Cardinals' defense unit returned to the field.

"What happened?" Joe asked as Tracy headed toward him at the sideline.

Coley, at Joe's side, said, "It's okay, it's okay."

Lew, approaching, asked, "How'd it happen?" Lew had been at the bottom of a pile of Marianna players who thought they had tackled the ball carrier.

Coach Holliman was down the sideline, frowning at the players on the field. His Cardinals were bracing again for defense, and the Marianna Panthers were lining up for their first play of the new series. In Coach Holliman's book, there was time later to dissect an error. The play coming up was the immediate problem.

Tracy looked stricken, almost panicky, as if

his worst fear had come true. "I had it, I had it," he said. "I caught the pass."

"I know," Joe said.

"But when I cut—brought the ball around to put it away—well, it just sailed out of my hands." Tracy looked at his hands as if he could not believe their betrayal. "And it was just gone, the ball was just gone."

A couple of players passing by slapped Tracy on the shoulder and said, "It's okay, we'll get 'em."

Each time, Tracy looked around to see who had spoken and to nod his appreciation.

Coley watched Tracy with a sympathetic expression, but said nothing.

"Were you hit?" Lew asked.

All the air seemed to go out of Tracy and he admitted, "No, I wasn't hit. I just lost it somehow."

"Not hit," Lew said. Lew, who held onto the ball while running over tacklers and tearing away from tacklers, sounded like he thought his ears were playing tricks on him.

"I said I wasn't hit," Tracy snapped. "It just got away from me."

Lew blinked at the outburst. "I didn't mean anything, Tracy," he said.

"Okay, okay," Joe said. "We had a flat practice week, and we've just got to concentrate more. We can do it. No problem." He turned to Tracy.

"You're not the first player to fumble, you know." He gave his friend a brief smile and stepped away from the three, down the sideline, as if to say, "Subject closed."

On the field, the stalled Marianna offense was lining up for its second punt of the game, and Coley dashed out to take up his position, back deep, to receive the ball.

Joe looked around for Coach Holliman and saw the coach stalking toward him to talk about the upcoming series of downs.

## Chapter 11

◆       "I've got to give the ball to Tracy right away," Joe said before the coach could speak. In other games, Joe had seen Coach Holliman bench a player for a bonehead play. The coach never held an excusable fumble against a player. But errors attributable to laziness or carelessness or lack of concentration were another matter. Joe wanted to forestall any such move against Tracy. "He'll be all right, once he handles the ball again," Joe added.

Coach Holliman aimed his frown at Joe. "You think so, eh?"

"Sure."

"I was thinking more in terms of leaving him on the bench. His mind was somewhere off in the stars, and it just didn't occur to him that maybe he ought to hold onto the ball until he got to the end zone."

Joe waited. He was not going to argue. First, the sideline during a game was neither the place nor the time for an argument. Beyond that, Joe knew that the Cardinals' quarterback was not going to win an argument on a judgment call with the Cardinals' coach.

Joe remembered the times—he couldn't count them—that Coach Holliman had said: "Always give the ball right back to a player who's fumbled. He needs to get his confidence back—and right away. And you can be sure he'll be trying harder to make up for the fumble."

On the field, the Marianna center snapped the ball.

Joe and Coach Holliman turned, not speaking, to watch the punt.

The linemen struggled at the line of scrimmage. None of the Cardinals' front-wall players succeeded in breaking through. The Marianna punter took the snap, stepped once, then once more, and kicked.

Coley circled under the high kick, watching the ball fall out of the darkness through the glare of the arc lights. At the last second, he raised a hand in signal of a fair catch and caught the ball on the Cardinals' thirty-three-yard line.

"Okay," Coach Holliman said.

Joe did not know whether the coach was referring to Coley's catch or approving Tracy for play in the upcoming series. Joe pulled on his helmet and leaned toward the coach as the kicking team and the offense unit changed places. Tracy was one of the players running onto the field.

"Keep it on the ground," Coach Holliman said. "We're bigger than they are. Grind it out and wear them down."

Joe nodded and started to pull away, then stopped and turned back when he heard the coach call his name.

"And, Joe, give the ball to Tracy—and tell him to hang onto it."

"Right, sure." Joe nodded and ran onto the field. Jogging toward the huddle forming around Charlie Garrison, Joe felt less of the nervousness, less of the frightening certainty that doom was right around the corner for the Hillcrest High Cardinals. Maybe his fears had foretold only one bit of doom—Tracy's fumble—and now everything was going to be all right.

In the huddle, Joe looked at Tracy and called his number for the first play. Tracy looked back at Joe with the expression of grim determination still in place, and gave a little nod.

Joe took the snap from center, faked a quick pitchout to Coley to the right, then whirled. Out of the corner of his eye he saw the blur of a white jersey—a Marianna lineman crashing through. He sent a hurried underhand spiral back to Tracy running to the left just as the lineman slammed into him.

Going down under the charge of the Marianna players, Joe knew with a feeling of horror that his pitchout had been off the mark. He had not given the sprinting Tracy enough lead. Tracy was going to have to slow his pace, perhaps reach back, to bring in the ball. Of all plays, why this one to go awry?

But when Joe scrambled free of the Marianna lineman and looked for Tracy, there he was, the ball tucked away in his right hand, spinning away from a tackler. He bounced off another tackler and battled his way forward to the forty-two-yard line where a low-hitting tackler pinned his knees together and brought him down. He had somehow gathered in the off-target pitchout and, with tough running, gained nine yards.

He wore a tight little smile of satisfaction when he joined the huddle.

Joe got the needed yard for the first down, and three more for good measure, on a quarterback sneak behind Charlie Garrison's block, moving the Cardinals to the Hillcrest High forty-six-yard line.

Lew gained six yards off tackle, crossing the midfield stripe, and then five through the middle for a first down on the Marianna forty-three-yard line.

With the four straight running plays, the Marianna linebackers were inching forward and closing the gap between them in the center. They were looking for more of Lew's thundering runs into the line.

On the next play Joe rifled a pass to the Cardinals' tight end, Benjy Moore, at the right sideline. Benjy caught the ball just before a Marianna defender arrived and knocked him out of bounds on the thirty-four-yard line.

With the nine-yard gain, the Cardinals faced second down and one yard to go for a first down, well inside Marianna territory. Joe weighed the alternatives. It was a good situation to waste a play, take a chance on a long pass to the end zone. If it clicked, the Cardinals had a touchdown. If it failed, the Cardinals still faced only third down with one yard to go, with a good chance of making the first down. Or, playing it safe, the Cardinals could go for the first down now and keep the drive alive.

Joe, a couple of steps away from the huddle, glanced at the sideline. Coach Holliman wasn't even looking at him. He was talking to Ike Murphy, one of the linebackers. The decision was Joe's.

Joe's lingering nervousness made up his mind for him. The Cardinals needed to score, and with as little risk as possible. In the huddle he called for himself to roll down the line and burst through off tackle for the needed yard for a first down.

He took the snap and turned and began moving down the line, to his right, keeping an eye on Coley swinging wide. A pitchout to Coley was his safety valve if a lineman broke through on him. Coley was also the decoy to lure the defensive end out wide, beyond reach of Joe breaking through off tackle.

Joe made his cut behind the right shoulder of the right tackle, Skip Matthews, and threw himself forward.

He saw Skip slide to the left, apparently unable to turn his opponent. The tackler came off Skip into Joe's path.

With the cut, Joe had committed himself. There was no chance of turning and pitching to Coley. Skip had let the tackler slip away at precisely the worst possible moment. A second earlier, Joe might have seen the threat and pitched out. A second later, it would not have mattered. Joe would have won his one-yard gain.

Joe lowered his left shoulder, planted his left foot, and drove forward with all his strength from his right foot.

He hit the tackler head-on. The tackler grabbed Joe around the shoulders and tried to shove him back. Joe lowered his right shoulder and drove forward with his left foot, and slipped past the tackler before going down.

He won the yard and the first down—but only barely.

Joe leaped to his feet, glaring at Skip.

Skip gave Joe a silly little smile and a shrug.

Joe said nothing.

Coley came up beside Joe on the way to the huddle. "Did Skip let that guy in on you?" he asked.

Joe turned to Coley, but what he saw in his mind was the sports page in the *St. Louis Journal-Gazette* with his name in a headline. What he heard, instead of Coley's voice, were the remarks of some of the linemen during the week.

"I hope not," Joe said to Coley as they reached the huddle.

Either way, Joe thought, Skip Matthews failed to move his opponent out of Joe's path. He cast a quick glance at Coach Holliman at the sideline and received in return only the familiar frown and glare.

Then the Marianna defense stiffened—or the Cardinals' attack faltered.

Lew got three yards over guard and Tracy plunged off tackle for two yards. Facing third down and five yards to go, Joe called a pass to Coley zigzagging to the right. Only Coley, letting his concentration waver at the critical moment, zigged when he should have zagged, and Joe's bullet pass went behind his back to the ground.

Joe stared at Coley in disbelief. The running back never made a mental error. But that was what had happened. Coley returned Joe's stare with every bit the same degree of disbelief.

"Sorry" was all he said as he ran past Joe to

the place where Charlie Garrison was setting up the huddle.

"Uh-huh," Joe said, turning to the sideline to look at Coach Holliman.

Now, with fourth down and five yards to go on the Marianna twenty-nine-yard line, Joe was looking for advice. The goalposts were ten yards beyond Harry Pearson's field goal range, leaving the Cardinals with two choices: try for the needed five yards for a first down with a run or a pass, or bring in Harry to try to punt the ball out of bounds near the goal line.

Coach Holliman was frowning at Coley, trying to figure out the cause of the lapse. Then he turned to Joe.

The coach gave Joe a barely discernible nod. That meant go for the first down. Then he held out his hands, palms down. That meant run, not pass. Then he held up a forefinger. One finger meant Joe.

Joe nodded. He understood.

When the Cardinals lined up, everybody in both bleachers stood.

Joe took the snap. He faked to Lew into the middle of the line. He pulled the ball back and turned to his right, cocking his arm quickly in the direction of Coley. Then he brought the ball back down, whirled, and ran wide to his left. Out in front of him, Tracy threw himself into the path of a tackler. They both crashed to the ground. For an instant, Joe saw a clear route to the goal. Then somebody crashed into his thigh. He spun and kept his feet. Then somebody else hit him waist high and he went down.

He was one yard short of the first down—and one block short of a touchdown.

Joe pulled off his helmet and jogged to the sideline.

At halftime the score stood at 0–0—a triumphant accomplishment for the supposedly hapless Marianna Panthers and a shocking disaster for the Hillcrest Cardinals.

The Panthers had yet to cross the fifty-yard line under their own steam but that was little consolation to a Hillcrest High team unable to cross the goal line. The Panthers, for all their weakness on the attack, had committed no costly errors—no fumbles, no pass interceptions.

In the dressing room, Coach Holliman, instead of his usual trek from one player to the next, criticizing and advising and encouraging, stood motionless against a wall, arms folded over his chest, surveying the collection of confused and frustrated faces.

"You have just played the worst half of a football game that any of you have ever seen," he said finally. "Perhaps even the worst that I've ever seen in my more than thirty years in this game."

Joe sat on a bench, elbows on his knees, hands clasped, staring at the floor. From his left he heard the slap-pause-slap of Lew subconsciously pounding his right fist into the palm of his left hand. There was no other sound in the dressing room.

Coach Holliman continued. "Next door, in the Panthers' dressing room, Coach Hawkins is telling the players—four-time losers, you know—that they can win this game, can knock off the highfalutin Hillcrest High Cardinals, the front runners in the Rend Lake Conference."

Joe looked up. He knew what was coming next.

"And Coach Hawkins is right. The Marianna Panthers, four-time losers, can whip the high-riding, cocksure Hillcrest Cardinals."

Joe wished Coach Holliman would quit referring to the Panthers as four-time losers.

Then, as if he had read Joe's mind, Coach Holliman said, "Four-time losers, and they're rubbing your faces in the dirt."

Coach Holliman's gaze moved from one player to the next, around the room.

Joe met the coach's eyes, then looked at Tracy. Tracy looked like he was in actual pain. His spectacular block for Joe and his strong running had not wiped away the horror of his fumble with only the goal line in front of him. Coley, next to Tracy, seemed tense, which was maybe good, maybe bad.

Joe's eyes met Skip Matthews's. Skip looked away. There had been no repeat of Skip's failure. But Joe could not forget Skip's silly grin.

"I've got pride, and my players have pride," Coach Holliman said. "If you don't take pride in what you do, you don't play for my team. We've got a tough second half coming up against a mediocre team that is now smelling victory. It's going to take extra effort—by players who have pride—for us to win this game."

He stopped, his mouth a straight line, his frown deep as ever. "Be forewarned," he said. "Any player giving less than his best—mentally and physically—is going to be seen as lacking sufficient pride to play for the Cardinals and will be pulled from the game, not just to the bench but to the dressing room. Finished."

Somebody behind Joe let out a soft, "Oooooh."

Joe looked at Skip, who was watching the coach.

"All right," Coach Holliman said. "Let's go."

The players got to their feet and shuffled single file through the door.

But from the moment that Coley gathered in the kickoff opening the second half, it was clear that a pep talk laced with a threat from Coach Holliman was not enough to make up for a poor practice week, a touch of overconfidence, and the smatterings of bad feelings produced by the *St. Louis Journal-Gazette*.

Coley took in the kick on the fifteen-yard line, then bobbled it like a juggler for a second.

Joe, watching from the sideline, felt his heart come up in his throat.

Finally, Coley got a grip on the ball. But he had lost valuable moments. The Marianna tacklers were bearing down on him.

Coley went into his jitterbug act, dodging one tackler, dancing away from another, spinning to freedom, and somehow made it to the twenty-seven-yard line.

Joe sent Lew into the line twice for gains of four and five yards, then handed off to Tracy off tackle for a three-yard gain and a first down on the thirty-nine-yard line.

He called a pass to Tracy, sending him angling inside and then reversing his field ten yards out and heading for the sideline.

Joe took the snap and rolled back without a fake. He heard the Marianna linebacker shout, "Pass!" He saw Tracy running toward the inside, with the defensive back trailing and a linebacker backpedaling to help cover him. Tracy suddenly cut, changing direction, and raced across the field.

The defensive back whirled, too. Being behind Tracy, he picked him up easily and was, actually, leading Tracy a bit. But Tracy was in front of him, between the defensive back and Joe.

Joe fired the ball at a spot in front of Tracy.

Joe knew instantly he was off the mark. He had led Tracy too much, maybe a step. And the pass was a shade too high.

But if Tracy could get a hand on the ball there was a good chance he would catch it.

Tracy stretched his right hand out, and did get his hand on the ball. But that was all. The pass, too high, glanced off his right hand and into the air and fell into the hands of the defensive back behind him.

The Marianna defensive back ran down the sideline to the end zone untouched.

# Chapter 12

◆ Joe glanced at the score-board behind the end zone to his right—Cardinals 0, Visitors 7. Hillcrest High was trailing for the first time since the opening-game loss to Morristown.

Then Joe looked to his left, at Coley getting set to receive the kickoff.

Standing at the sideline, his helmet cradled in his right hand like a runner carrying a football, Joe unconsciously nodded his head. He tried to think positively, think victory, think success. Forget the interception. Forget Tracy's fumble. Forget Coley zigging when he should have zagged on the pass pattern. Forget the suspicions about Skip's missed block. Forget all the bad. Think good.

The bleachers behind him and across the field were silent except for the scattered shouts of the few Marianna fans loyal enough to a four-time loser to make the trip to Hillcrest. The Cardinals' fans, accustomed to victory, seemed stunned.

Joe no longer felt the nervousness that had troubled him in the afternoon and into the opening minutes of the game. That was good. That was one good thing. What was another?

Well, Marianna was leading on the scoreboard, it was true, but the fact remained that the Panthers had not yet moved beyond the fifty-yard line under their own power. The touchdown was scored by the defense. Their offense was sputtering in the face of the Cardinals' tough defenders. That was a good sign. What else?

The Cardinals were moving on offense. But for a fluke of a fumble by Tracy, they would have scored on their first possession. But for the lack of a single block, Joe would have scored on the fourth-down run. Lew was chewing up yardage. So was Tracy. The Cardinals were sure to score. That was all good news.

Joe recalled Coach Holliman's advice in the first quarter: "We're bigger than they are. We can wear 'em down." So time was on the side of the larger, stronger Hillcrest High Cardinals. And that was good news.

Okay, Joe thought. Okay. He was eager for the kickoff and the opportunity to try again.

The Marianna kicker, probably getting in the mood of victory, backed Coley up to the ten-yard line with a booming kick down the middle.

Coley caught the ball and ran straight up the middle of the field. No jitterbugging, no spinning and dodging, no wriggling around, just a straight race toward a crowd of his teammates in the middle of the field at the thirty-yard line.

Coley, turning on the speed, made it to the twenty, then the twenty-five, and disappeared into the crowd of Cardinals between the thirty and the forty. Then, a moment later, he popped out of the other side of the crowd, shaking off the hand of a tackler.

The Hillcrest High fans in the bleachers on both sides of the field suddenly came to life. Coley's electrifying run brought them to their feet now with a roaring cheer.

Skip materialized out of nowhere and threw himself in front of two tacklers and Coley dashed across the fifty-yard line.

Only one remaining Marianna player, off to the right and now dashing toward Coley, offered a threat. Coley spotted him and veered to his left, trying to put distance between himself and his pursuer. With the advantage of the angle, Coley crossed the goal at the corner with the Marianna tackler still ten yards behind him.

Coley tossed the ball to the referee and, hands raised high, raced toward the bench, a wide grin on his face.

Joe rushed forward to meet him, and grabbed him in a hug at the twenty-yard line. Yes, thought Joe, swinging Coley around, think good, think success. Then they both were engulfed in a swarm of players.

While Coley and most of the others moved on toward the bench, Joe turned and ran onto the field to take up his duties as holder for the kick for extra point.

Harry Pearson kicked good and the scoreboard showed: Cardinals 7, Visitors 7.

But the Marianna Panthers were far from finished.

So close to a victory that would turn their lackluster season into a success, they battled ferociously on every play. The Cardinals battled back, and the two teams rocked through the third quarter without either allowing the other to mount a serious threat. On their second possession, the Panthers did drive across the fifty-yard line under their own power for the first time. But on the next play their ball carrier, bouncing off tackle, fumbled and the Cardinals recovered. For Hillcrest High, Lew's punishing runs into the line and Joe's skilled running of the option kept the Cardinals moving, but never quite enough to gain the end zone.

As the teams changed ends of the field for the start of the fourth quarter, Joe noticed in walking past the Marianna defenders the unmistakable signs of weariness. There was no spring in their step, and a lot of them were puffing.

The Cardinals, with second down and five yards to go for a first down, lined up at their own forty-one-yard line for the first play of the fourth quarter. Joe scanned the defense, took the snap, and—once again—handed off to the powerhouse Lew, who tore into the middle of the line.

Lew broke through, bumped his way past a tired linebacker, spun, and pounded his way nine yards to the fifty for a first down. From there, Joe pitched out to Coley for six yards, and sent Tracy around end for seven and yet another first down.

The Hillcrest High fans, sensing that now, finally, the time had come for the Cardinals to drive to the end zone and take the lead, were on their feet in the bleachers.

Joe, too, knew that the Cardinals were taking command of the game, and he sensed the feeling among his teammates.

From the thirty-seven-yard line, Joe rolled out and gained six yards around right end, then fired a pass to Benjy Moore over the middle for seven yards to the twenty-four-yard line, and the Marianna coach called for a time-out.

Joe jogged to the sideline to meet with Coach Holliman.

The coach was frowning—what else?—but the angry glare of the halftime intermission was gone from his eyes. "Steady as she goes," he said. "Keep it simple. We need this touchdown."

"Uh-huh." Joe looked at the scoreboard clock. Already, almost four minutes of the fourth quarter had ticked away.

On the first play after the time-out, Joe threw to Tracy racing for the left corner. Tracy took in the pass on the five-yard line, held on when a Marianna tackler slammed into him, and fell across the goal line.

Harry's kick wobbled off to the left, no good, and the scoreboard stood at: Cardinals 13, Visitors 7.

But the scoreboard numbers did not stand for long.

The Marianna kickoff receiver fumbled when tackled at the twenty-one-yard line on the return, and Hillcrest High recovered.

Then Joe, on the first play, took the snap and moved down the line to his right. He glanced at Coley, drifting near the sideline, ready for a pitchout. Then Joe put the ball away and cut through right tackle. Skip succeeded this time in forcing his opponent out of Joe's path. Joe burst through the opening. Coley, racing across, caused a much larger linebacker enough trouble to allow Joe to gallop past him. Then Joe cut back and outran the defensive backs to the end zone.

This time, Harry kicked good: 20–7.

* * *

And that was the score at the finish, 20–7, when the Cardinals—with more of a sense of relief than victory—trooped into their dressing room. There was no cheering, no whooping, no shouting. There were no slaps on the back, no flying towels with howls of laughter. It might have been the losers' dressing room.

"Lucky," Joe said to nobody in particular as he dropped onto the bench in front of his locker for a moment before peeling off his uniform and pads and heading to the shower.

Coley was right behind Joe and he began undressing without delay. "We should've beat those guys by fifty points," he said.

Joe gave a little laugh. "Maybe," he said, "if we had started playing earlier. It's like we weren't there the first half."

Coley stared at Joe for a long moment. "You know, you're the one who did it—kept us in the game, and then pulled it out." He spoke the words slowly, as if weighing each before saying it.

"Me? You're the one who ran back a kickoff to tie the score and get us going. And Lew—he was really stomping. Tracy caught the go-ahead touchdown pass."

Coley finished undressing. "No, it was you," he said, and walked off to the showers with a towel around his waist.

Joe watched him go, then took a deep breath, leaned back against his locker, and exhaled. Without willing it, he recalled the line in the *St. Louis Journal-Gazette* story: "How good might Joe Mitchell be if . . . ?" If Tracy hadn't fumbled. If Coley had been where Joe expected him to be on the pass. If Skip Matthews had made his block. If, if, if.

Joe shook his head and bent down to untie his shoestrings and pull off the cleated shoes. Then he got to his feet and began taking off his jersey.

Joe's parents were watching a movie on television in the living room when he walked through the front door. They looked at him with surprise. He was home earlier than usual for a game night.

Joe, Coley, Tracy, and Lew had stopped by the usual postgame party in the gym. It was almost required duty for the players to put in an appearance after a game. But they left while the party was still in full swing. And, without anyone voicing the suggestion, all seemed to assume that this was not a night for reliving the game at Tracy's house. They had won, but did not feel triumphant. Tracy dropped off Lew, then Coley, then Joe. At each stop, there was a round of "Good night" and "See you tomorrow," and nothing else.

"You're early," Joe's mother said. "There's nothing wrong, is there?"

Joe grinned at her concern. "No, nothing's wrong."

"That was scary out there tonight," his father said.

"Yeah, scary," Joe said.

"What was wrong?"

"Everything," Joe said. "I'm going to bed."

In his room, Joe stood at the window, hands thrust in the hip pockets of his jeans, and stared out at the darkness.

His father had used the right word—"scary."

Fortunately, the Cardinals were able to afford all those errors against the Marianna Panthers and still win.

But now, just one week away, there were the undefeated Hoytville Cougars and the title game of the Rend Lake Conference, all of which was quite another matter.

For one more week, Joe had to block out thoughts of Randolph University and Ryder State and the backfield package. He had to concentrate on winning one more game with the Hillcrest High Cardinals.

# Chapter 13

Joe awoke on Saturday morning to the sound of large raindrops splattering on the window of his room. He lifted his head and glanced at the window. The dark clouds foretold a full day or more of rain. Behind the rain would come colder weather, he knew. In southern Illinois, rain rather than snow was the usual harbinger of winter.

Joe swung himself around and put his feet on the cold floor. He rubbed the sleep out of his eyes and then for a moment watched the rain hit the glass pane.

For Joe and the Hillcrest High Cardinals football team, rain meant trouble. Hillcrest High had no field house for indoor football drills. Practice on a mud-slick field was dangerous, risking injury in the simplest of plays. Coach Holliman sometimes took the Cardinals inside to the basketball court, with the players wearing sweat suits and tennis shoes, for practice on rainy days. But the hardwood floor prohibited any contact, and the space restrictions made the workouts practically useless.

With the game against the Hoytville Cougars looming on the horizon, the Cardinals were going to need every moment of practice. They not only had to hone to perfection their standard plays, but undoubtedly there were going to be a few new plays—"new wrinkles," Coach Holliman called them—to learn.

Joe heaved a sigh and rubbed a bruise on his thigh. But this was only Saturday. Maybe the rain would stop before Monday.

He stood up and grabbed a robe for warmth against the chill of the room. He pulled on the robe and walked out of his room and down the stairs to the kitchen.

"Are you all right?" his mother asked. She always asked that on the morning after a game.

"Yeah, fine. Dad's already gone?"

"Uh-huh. He'll be back about noon."

Joe's father almost always spent his Saturday mornings at his office. He insisted he could get more work done in half a day in an empty office on Saturday morning than in two business days crowded with people and ringing telephones.

Joe stretched and felt again the bruise on his thigh. His eye fell on the *St. Louis Journal-*

*Gazette*, folded on the breakfast table. He glanced at the front page without reading any of the words in the headlines, and felt a twinge. He wondered if he would ever be able to look at the newspaper without recalling the excitement, then embarrassment, he had felt when reading about himself last Sunday.

"I'll get dressed," he said.

"I'll have breakfast for you when you come back down."

Joe's mother placed a platter of French toast and bacon, a glass of orange juice, and a glass of milk in front of him. "You won't have to wash Tracy's van this morning," she said with a smile and a nod toward the window.

Joe grinned at her. "See, a gloomy day is not all bad." Then he added, "And Coley loves rainy Saturdays. The ice cream dipping business falls off to nothing. And Lew, too. He gets out of working if his father had something outdoors scheduled."

He dug into the breakfast, and was half finished when the telephone rang.

"It's Tracy," his mother said. "Do you want me to tell him you're eating and will call him back?"

"No," Joe said, shoving his chair back and getting to his feet. "I'll make it quick."

Joe walked across the room and accepted the telephone from his mother. "Hey," he said, and started to add that he was eating breakfast and couldn't talk for long.

But Tracy didn't let Joe get the second word out. "Great news!" he boomed.

Joe blinked. He remembered the Tracy Jackson of the night before—the grim determination on his face before the game, the stunned expression when he fumbled away a sure touchdown, the somber mood after the game—and couldn't imagine what had happened. "Huh? What?" Joe finally said.

"My dad says we can visit Ryder State, too, along with the schools on that list of his."

Joe did not know whether to grin or frown. For the sake of the Hoytville game, he wanted to grin. Tracy, exuberant, was back to normal. But if he was making progress in talking his father into allowing him to go to Ryder State, Joe was facing the prospect of being left on his own with the choice: keep the deal on the backfield package, or break it. With that thought, Joe realized that his commitment to the backfield package going to Ryder State was slipping away. The realization gave him an uneasy feeling. Joe wound up frowning at the telephone and said, "Good."

"Good? It's great. Don't you see?"

Joe hesitated, thinking. Then he said, "Yeah, that's what I meant—good—great."

Tracy wasn't sure that Joe understood.

"Look," he said, lowering his voice. "After all the visiting is done, I say, 'Look, I like Ryder State.' And what can he say?"

Joe was able to think of several things that Tracy's father might say. But he knew that Tracy almost always got his way on everything in the end. Joe thought of the Hoytville game, and tried to block out everything else. For the sake of the game, this was good news. He said, "Okay," with as much of an upbeat lilt as he could manage. Then, with a small laugh, he added, "If you say so."

"Your breakfast is getting cold," Joe's mother announced from across the kitchen.

Joe nodded at her.

"You don't sound very enthused," Tracy said. "Is Coley right that you're really thinking about—"

Joe cut him off. "Wait a minute. Look, I'm eating breakfast. Let me call you back, okay?"

There was a long silence from Tracy's end of the line. Then he said, "Oh, sure. Okay."

"Talk to you later."

"Right."

Joe hung up the telephone slowly. Yes, it should have been great news, a ray of hope for the backfield package. But Joe was beginning to face the fact that his own hope was that Tracy's father was going to provide Joe with a way out of the deal. But now, maybe not. Look, it's a ray of hope for the Hoytville game, so take it and be grateful. Time to worry about other things later.

Joe shrugged unconsciously as he turned from the telephone and returned to the breakfast table.

"Is anything wrong?" his mother asked.

Joe wished, for probably the thousandth time, that his mother was not so able to pick up his signals.

"No, no," Joe said. "I'm not sure what it means, but Tracy says his father has agreed to visit Ryder State as one of the schools Tracy can choose from. Tracy thinks he's got it made now, going to Ryder State with the rest of us."

Joe's mother watched him. "And you've been pulling for Tracy's father, to get you out of the deal."

Joe looked at his mother and shook his head. "I don't know," he said.

Joe finished his breakfast and, in short order, two more telephone calls came in before he could return Tracy's call.

The first was from Coach Holliman.

Could Joe meet the coach at the school to go over some of the information he had gathered about the Hoytville High Cougars?

This was something new. Coach Holliman

had never called Joe in on a weekend to talk about an upcoming opponent. Was Hoytville really that tough? Well, yes. Was the Rend Lake Conference championship really that important? Yes, for sure.

Joe said, "Sure. When?"

"As soon as you can. I'm at the school now. I'm going to have a couple of the boys from the defense come in later."

Joe glanced at the rain hitting the kitchen window and reflected that his father had the family car parked in the lot at the Hillcrest Water Works, and would have it there until around noon. It meant a long walk in the rain. Well, he had a raincoat and an umbrella. He said, "Sure, I'll be there in a few minutes."

"Thank you," Coach Holliman said in his formal way.

Joe was explaining to his mother where he was going and why, when the telephone rang again.

The voice of Coley Brewster demanded to know if Joe did not think Tracy's news was the greatest ever.

Then Coley waited, and Joe could sense in the silence Coley's suspicions.

Joe weighed his words carefully. "Well, it's certainly a step in turning Tracy's dad around," he said. "From that standpoint, yeah, it was great news, and I'm happy for Tracy and I hope now he can quit worrying about it and concentrate on the Hoytville Cougars."

Joe took a breath, satisfied with the way he had stated his view. He wanted to turn the conversation away from Ryder State and back to the Hoytville game.

But he hadn't succeeded.

"Tracy said you were kind of cool," Coley said.

"Cool? He called while I was eating my breakfast. I wanted to finish my breakfast." He paused. "What's going on here?"

"Nothing, I guess," Coley said.

Joe decided to pass up the obvious invitation to offer all sorts of lengthy reassurances. "Look, Coley, I just got a call from Coach Holliman. I've got to meet him at the school to go over some stuff on Hoytville. Like right now. I'll talk to you later. Okay?"

Coach Holliman's move was a new one to Coley, too. "Coach Holliman . . . ?" he said, puzzled.

"Coley, I think Coach Holliman thinks Hoytville is going to be a tough game. Understand? Look, really, I've got to go. I'll fill you in later."

"Yeah," Coley said.

Joe took a breath, glanced at his wristwatch, and dialed Tracy's number. Tracy already had reported to Coley and probably to Lew, too, that Joe had not sounded happy enough with his news. If Joe didn't call him back, there was no telling what his friends in the backfield would be telling one another—and with the Hoytville Cougars coming up.

"Hey," he said when Tracy answered the telephone. "I'd have gotten back to you quicker but this phone hasn't stopped ringing."

"Yeah, it's okay."

Joe subconsciously raised an eyebrow at Tracy's tone. It was clear that Tracy, too, now had growing suspicions that Joe was not going to be a part of the backfield package at Ryder State.

Joe quickly explained the call from Coach Holliman, and then said, "We'll get together this evening. I'll fill you in on what he says. Call the others, will you?"

He hung up the telephone, got his rain gear, opened the front door, and then turned back to call out, "I'm gone."

Fortunately, there was no wind, so the rain, although heavy, was falling straight down. Joe, his raincoat buttoned, held the umbrella close to his head, walking the familiar route to Hillcrest High.

He was thankful for the meeting with the coach. It enabled him to avoid Tracy and Coley and Lew during the morning, and the inevitable talk about Tracy's triumph. Also, it served to focus his mind—and the minds of the others, too, when they met later—on the Hoytville High Cougars.

He walked briskly, resisting the urge to jog. If he trotted, with the raincoat flapping around and the umbrella being pulled out of position, he was sure to arrive soaking wet.

He took a little jump off a curb to avoid a puddle of water and walked toward the last corner before Hillcrest High.

At the corner, he waited while a car passed. The driver honked and waved, but did not stop and offer him a ride. Joe could not see through the rainswept windows who the driver was, and he did not recognize the car. He assumed that the driver thought Joe was headed for the high school, just ahead.

Joe cut across the parking lot and pulled open the door leading to the basement and Coach Holliman's office. In the darkened corridor, Joe closed the umbrella and slipped out of his raincoat. He heard low voices and wondered who was with Coach Holliman in his office.

At the door, Joe saw only Coach Holliman, seated behind his old metal desk.

"Come in, Joe," the coach said.

Stepping through the door, Joe saw the other man. He was seated on a straight chair against the wall. Joe knew him—everyone in Hillcrest did—but stared in puzzlement and then cast a questioning look at Coach Holliman.

"You know Mr. Abbott, of course," Coach Holliman said.

"Sure," Joe said. Henry Abbott was an attorney in Hillcrest. More to the point, he had played end for the Hillcrest High Cardinals and, later, for Southern Illinois University.

Henry Abbott nodded a greeting to Joe.

"Have a seat, Joe," Coach Holliman said, gesturing at the only other chair in the small office.

Joe hung the umbrella and the raincoat on the wooden coat tree in the corner and sat down.

"Mr. Abbott watched the Hoytville Cougars in their last two games, Joe," Coach Holliman said. "And he has learned some very interesting things."

# Chapter 14

For an hour Joe, his chair pulled up close to Coach Holliman's desk, listened to Henry Abbott and watched him draw diagrams with a pencil on sheets of typewriter paper.

As each diagram was completed, and the discussion ended, Mr. Abbott slid the paper across to Joe, glanced at a page in a small spiral notebook, and began again.

He outlined the Hoytville defenses he had seen. He drew the Cougars' lineup for a goal-line stand. He penciled in the slight changes the Cougars used in a short-yardage situation. Joe would see them line up that way, he said, if he was trying to run on fourth down with one yard to go. There were others—the positions the Cougars took when a pass was expected, when an end run or a pitchout or a rollout was expected.

Mr. Abbott detailed the unconscious moves he had seen tipping off whether the Cougars were going to rush a punter and try to block the kick, or drop back and block for their punt returner.

Then the lawyer-turned-scout analyzed the Hoytville team position by position, player by player.

The Hoytville forward wall was huge and hard to move. Lew was going to have a tough night, and probably not a very successful one, plunging into the line. But one hopeful tip: The right side of the line was markedly stronger than the left. So hit the left side of the line more often.

The two linebackers were rangy and strong. The one backing up the left side of the line knew that his side of the front wall was the weaker one, and he tended to move in to help at the first sign of a ball carrier going there. That left space open behind him for Joe to pass, if he could fool the linebacker with a fake to Lew. The line-backer behind the right side of the line tended to tip off his intention to blitz by standing with his left foot slightly forward; otherwise, he stood with his feet in a straight line.

"You're going to love the defensive back on the right side," Mr. Abbott said. "He's a weak link, slow and unsure of himself. The one on the left is pretty good. He picked off two passes in one of the games I saw."

Mr. Abbott was jotting notes on his dia-grams—"leaps forward" for the linebacker behind the left side of the line, "left foot out to blitz" for the other linebacker.

Repeatedly referring to his spiral notebook, he always identified a player in his diagram by number, and sometimes referred to him by number in talking as well—54 does this and 41 does that.

Joe was a running quarterback, capable of scrambling, and that was good, Mr. Abbott said, "because that big line is going to be breaking through on you a lot. You're going to have to throw on the run quite a bit."

But the big line had its drawbacks. "They're big and strong, but not quick," Mr. Abbott said. "You can sucker them on a draw play, and they'll be slow to recover. On the option, if you can make them commit to you, a pitchout to Coley ought to go a long, long way."

Joe watched the scribbling pencil, and glanced up from time to time to meet Mr. Abbott's eyes and nod his understanding.

For the most part, Coach Holliman remained quiet, leaning back in his chair, letting Mr. Abbott tell Joe what he knew. It was clear to Joe that the coach already had heard it all. He probably had heard most of it a week ago, following the lawyer's first trip to watch the Hoytville Cougars, and had had time to digest the information. Knowing Joe better than Mr. Abbott, Coach Holliman broke in occasionally with an encouraging remark, "You can do that," and, "You're strong in that type of play."

Abruptly, Mr. Abbott closed his spiral notebook, poked his pencil in his jacket pocket, leaned back, and fixed an unsmiling gaze on Joe. "That's it," he said. "Any questions?"

Joe shook his head. He glanced at Coach Holliman and then back at Mr. Abbott. It seemed to Joe that this amateur scout, a lawyer who once played for the Cardinals, now doing a favor for his former coach, had collected a remarkable array of details. Joe tapped the stack of papers on the desk. "May I take these pages?" he asked.

Mr. Abbott finally gave his first smile. "You certainly may."

Joe was at the outside door, his raincoat on and buttoned, beginning to open the umbrella, when Coach Holliman appeared in the far end of the corridor. He waved and said, "Joe, a minute."

Joe lowered the unopened umbrella and watched the coach walking toward him.

"Is everything all right?" Coach Holliman asked when he stopped in front of Joe.

"Sure," Joe said, almost automatically. He was certain that Coach Holliman was asking about the distractions that plagued the Cardinals in the Marianna game. But, if possible, Joe was going to avoid talking about it. So he added,

"Mr. Abbott was very clear on all the points. I got it all, and I understood it. I'll give it a lot of study, and—"

"That's not what I meant, Joe."

"Huh?"

"It didn't go well last night. I thought for a while we were not going to be able to pull it out. Not with you being obviously nervous about something, Tracy so absentminded he couldn't even hold onto the football, and Coley forgetting which way to run on a pass pattern, and . . ." He let the sentence trail off, convinced he had set the subject straight and now was ready to hear what Joe had to say.

Joe nodded slightly, thinking. He was going to have to answer the coach. "It's going to be okay," he said. "Tracy was worried about his dad not even considering Ryder State. But he told me this morning that his dad has agreed to take a look at Ryder State, and that everything is going to be fine."

Coach Holliman frowned at Joe a moment without speaking. Then he said, "And you, Joe, do you consider that to be fine?"

Joe clamped his lips tightly together and hesitated. The coach was asking for an answer that Joe was having trouble giving even to himself. He finally said, "Honestly, I don't know."

"I think you do know," Coach Holliman snapped right back at him.

Joe waited. Yes, he thought, he did know. The thought, coming so easily to mind, surprised him.

"Looking around—at Randolph and maybe some other schools—is the best thing for you in the long run. Randolph is a great university, and they're interested in you. There may be others. Taking a look around is the only thing that makes sense for you."

Joe nodded. The coach was right, he knew. But, still . . .

"You need to face that fact," Coach Holliman said. "If you face that fact, you can put the whole question behind you and concentrate on the Hoytville game."

Joe nodded again but did not speak.

Abruptly, Coach Holliman changed the subject. "Did any of them—Coley, Tracy, Lew—say anything about the story in the *St. Louis Journal-Gazette*?"

Joe frowned. "Nothing really," he said. "Just some kidding, you know."

"I'm afraid that some took it seriously," Coach Holliman said, watching Joe.

Joe remembered the look on Skip Matthews's face after the missed block early in the Marianna game but said nothing.

"I'll have a talk with Skip and a couple of others," Coach Holliman said.

Joe was sure his face went white. He wasn't

surprised that Coach Holliman had noticed the missed block. Very little on a football field escaped the coach. But Joe did not want Skip or any of the linemen to think he had complained. He said, "Oh, no, no, please. I'm sure that Skip thought, well, this was Marianna, and he could afford to slip once. He won't do that against Hoytville, no matter how he feels. I'm sure."

Coach Holliman watched Joe for a moment, then nodded and said, "All right."

The rain was easing up but still falling as Joe walked home with Mr. Abbott's diagrams and notes stuffed in his jeans pocket, his left hand jammed in his raincoat pocket, his right hand holding the umbrella low over his head.

But Joe's thoughts were not on the penciled notes, and he was barely aware of the rain.

Only now did he really realize that he had silently—silently but consciously—agreed with Coach Holliman. The coach said that Joe should consider other schools, without the backfield package. And Joe had told himself that he knew the coach was right. Then the coach said Joe needed to face the fact of what was the best thing for him to do. And Joe had, silently, faced the fact.

"I'm going to look at Randolph, and I'm going to consider any other school that looks like a possibility," Joe said in a whisper. Then, to himself, he added, "There, I've said it."

He took a deep breath. He smiled at the rain. He felt like a heavy load had been lifted off his back.

But, for sure, there was no need to say it to anyone else before the Hoytville game was behind them.

Walking the last block toward home, Joe saw his father turn the car into the driveway, get out, and jog the few steps through the rain to the front porch. Then he disappeared into the house.

Joe walked the remaining steps and stopped on the porch, taking off the dripping raincoat and draping it over one of the wicker porch chairs. He laid the soaked umbrella on the porch floor.

Inside, he called out, "Home," and then before anyone could answer, he added, "I've got to call the guys right away."

He dialed Coley first, hoping to catch him before he left for work at the drugstore.

"What'd Coach Holliman want?" Coley asked before Joe could speak.

Joe explained Mr. Abbott's scouting assignment, and the crash course he had given Joe on the Hoytville Cougars' defenses, and said, "We've got to get together, all of us."

"I've got to go to work in a minute."

"I know. But what about tonight, or tomorrow afternoon?"

Coley gave a little snort and said, "Tracy's got a date for some party at the Hillcrest Country Club tonight."

"Okay, tomorrow afternoon. I'll give him a call, and Lew."

Joe next dialed Tracy, filled him in, and set the date for Sunday afternoon.

It was just as well that Tracy had a date for a party. Lew was out on a job with his father and the time of their return was uncertain. So Lew's father did have an inside job—painting a room or putting in kitchen cabinets—to occupy them on this rainy day. Joe knew from experience with Lew that inside jobs did not have to end when darkness fell, as the outside jobs did. A flick of the light switch and they were ready to continue. Sometimes Lew did not get free of an inside job until ten o'clock. Joe left a message with Lew's mother.

He hung up the telephone and pulled the folded pages out of his jeans pocket as he walked to the kitchen.

He dropped the pages on the table and said to his father, "Everything you need to know about the Hoytville Cougars."

"Oh?"

Joe explained the session with Mr. Abbott in Coach Holliman's office.

Joe's father looked up at him with a grin and said, "And, at this very moment, some player in Hoytville is arriving at his home with everything you need to know about the Hillcrest High Cardinals."

Joe frowned. "Ouch," he said. "I never thought of that."

Joe picked up Coley and Lew early on Sunday afternoon and they went to Tracy's house. The rain, having continued through Saturday night, was dying away to a drizzle.

Then the four of them spent the afternoon in Tracy's den poring over and discussing Henry Abbott's notes. They memorized the jersey numbers of the key Hoytville players, and matched them to the strengths and weaknesses cited in the scouting notes.

To Joe's relief, nobody made the first mention of Ryder State, Randolph, or any other school that might be in the future of any one of them. When Tracy's father came in for a word of greeting, and then stayed a few minutes to look over the markings on the sheets of paper and listen to the discussion, Joe cast an apprehensive look at Tracy. But Tracy was concentrating on the notes, and neither he nor his father mentioned their talks—maybe arguments—about colleges during the past week. Coley, glancing from Tracy to his father and back again, seemed to be expecting one or the other to mention the subject. For a scary moment, Joe thought Coley was going to bring it up. But he didn't.

Instead, they all talked about Hoytville—the big linemen who were going to give Lew trouble and were going to break through on Joe trying to pass, the linebackers' tendencies, the two defensive backs with their varying degrees of ability.

"You know," Joe said at one point, recalling his father's remark, "the Hoytville players are probably studying us right now—Lew's a strong fullback, Coley's quick and slippery, Tracy knows how to catch a pass."

"Yeah," Coley said in wonder, the thought dawning on him for the first time. "If Coach Holliman had somebody scouting them, they maybe—no, probably—had somebody scouting us, too."

Tracy grinned. "If they scouted us against Marianna, they're probably suffering from an acute case of overconfidence right now," he said.

"I don't even want to talk about the Marianna game," Joe said.

When they broke up, with Coley and Lew piling into Joe's car for the ride home, the rain had stopped and the sky was clearing.

## Chapter 15

◆          From the start, the practice week was like none Joe had seen before. Coach Holliman gave fair warning that this was going to be a different kind of week when he hailed the players around him on the practice field at the start of the Monday drill.

"As you know," he said, standing in the center of the ring of players, "no team has ever won the Rend Lake Conference championship two years in a row." He turned slowly as he spoke. "By defeating Hoytville on Friday night, you will become the first team ever to win back-to-back championships."

Joe noticed that the coach said "will become," not "can become." There simply was no "if" in Coach Holliman's vocabulary.

Then Joe thought that the elderly coach probably wanted the victory and the championship even more than he was showing. This might be his last chance. There might never be another

Hillcrest High Cardinals team with this measure of strength and talent—the backfield package of four seniors operating behind a tough and experienced forward wall. Graduation was going to take a heavy toll. Next year was not going to be a championship season for the Cardinals. And, surely, Coach Holliman did not have a lot of seasons left before retirement.

"We've always won by excelling in the basics—blocking, tackling, running, passing," Coach Holliman told the players. "Nothing fancy, just good, solid football. And that's what is going to beat Hoytville on Friday night."

Joe shifted his weight from one foot to the other. He had heard the coach's speech about the basics before. Everyone had.

"But to help us succeed with the basics against Hoytville, we're going to mix in a few surprises."

Surprises? Joe, alert now, watched Coach Holliman. Almost every week, Coach Holliman added what he liked to call "new wrinkles." These were minor variations on the Cardinals' standard plays—Coley lining up out wider, Tracy taking on a new blocking assignment, Lew receiving pitchouts. They were small changes designed to unsettle the opponent's defense a bit, giving the Cardinals a slight edge. They were not changes that anyone would call a "surprise." Joe waited.

"We're going to add some new and different

plays to complicate life for the Hoytville Cougars," Coach Holliman said.

He had the attention of all the players now.

Typically, before moving on with an explanation of the new and different plays, the coach issued a note of caution. "But as we work on these new plays," he said, "I want you to understand that we are not abandoning the style of football that brought us this far. That would be dumb."

He turned again and looked beyond the players encircling him—first at one sideline, then the other. There was nobody in sight. Seldom did anyone show up to watch the Cardinals in practice. Coach Holliman was just making sure that if anyone was standing around and watching, it was a familiar face, not a visitor from Hoytville.

Then he spoke again. There were three plays, he said—a double reverse, a halfback pass, and a tackle eligible play.

"They are unlike anything we've ever done," he said. "More to the point, they are unlike anything the Hoytville Cougars will be expecting."

Joe thought again of his father's remark about Hoytville scouting the Cardinals, and concluded that Coach Holliman also was assuming Hoytville High had sent someone to watch the Cardinals.

"For these plays to provide maximum benefit,

they must be surprises, so don't tell your visiting Uncle Joe and Aunt Martha from Hoytville about them."

Coach Holliman paused for the small ripple of laughter from the players.

"Matter of fact," he said, "don't even tell your family and friends here in Hillcrest. Let's surprise our fans, too."

Through the week the Cardinals pounded their way through the practice sessions, business as usual, with the occasional break to run one of the new plays.

Each time, Coach Holliman unexpectedly stopped the drill, said, "Okay, hear this," and then looked around for a face at the sideline that might be from Hoytville before telling the offense which play to run.

The double reverse play had Joe handing off to Tracy running right, then Tracy handing off to Coley running left, and finally Coley handing off to Joe, who knifed off tackle and headed for the sideline. The threat of Coley jitterbugging in an open field was enough to lure the lumbering Hoytville defenders to the left while Joe ran to the right. Remembering Mr. Abbott's report that the big Hoytville linemen were slow to shift direction, Joe figured the play was sure to be a big gainer.

Joe got a surprise the first time the players

walked through the halfback pass play. Joe was the receiver. He had never caught a pass in a game in his life. Joe always was the thrower, not the receiver, of passes. But the thrower in this new play was Tracy, who had never thrown a pass in a game. So here they were, Joe handing off to Tracy and drifting out into the left flat while Tracy ran to the right. Then, on the same count, Tracy slammed on the brakes, turned, and cocked his arm to pass, and Joe broke into a sprint down the field. With luck, the play had touchdown written all over it.

And Skip Matthews got a surprise in the first rehearsal of the tackle eligible play. The Cardinals' right tackle, who was known to complain about slugging it out in the trenches while the quarterback got the glory, was the designated ball carrier. This did not seem to surprise him. But he went wide-eyed when he learned that Joe Mitchell was leading the blocking for him.

Joe grinned at Skip and said, "Just follow me."

Skip was strong enough to make the play go, Joe was sure, if his inexperience in handling the football didn't lead to a fumble.

The Cardinals ran the plays in full-speed contact scrimmage on Wednesday, and Joe saw for the first time that there were bad as well as good possibilities. With the element of surprise, each of the plays offered the chance of a huge gain, if not a touchdown. But each of them also risked large losses of yardage, or worse.

The double reverse required time to work, and so did the halfback pass. One lineman bursting through could set the Cardinals back ten yards or more. In the tackle eligible play, one lineman spotting Skip as eligible to carry the ball could stop him in his tracks. Beyond that danger, the tackle eligible play did put the ball in Skip's untried hands.

Gambling on dangerous plays was very unlike Coach Holliman. But, Joe figured, maybe that was what the Hoytville Cougars would think, too, enabling the plays to work.

All through the practice week, the intensity of the drills and the excitement of the new plays kept everyone's attention focused on the Hoytville game.

The four friends, whether gathered in the lobby before classes or eating lunch in the cafeteria or walking home in the darkness after practice, talked about Joe blocking for Skip, Tracy passing to Joe, Coley's role in the double reverse.

Nobody made the first mention of the backfield package, Ryder State, or Randolph University.

Coach Holliman said nothing more to Joe about his plans, and Joe said nothing to anyone.

* * *

Off the field, in the corridors of Hillcrest High and half a mile away in downtown Hillcrest, out at the mall on the highway to Carbondale, and at Happy Andy's hamburger stand at the edge of town—everywhere, banners and posters in the Hillcrest High colors of cardinal and white began appearing at midweek.

A huge banner in the lobby of Hillcrest High said: "Beat Hoytville."

The banner across the main street of the town said: "Go Cardinals."

Some shop windows were painted, the best being Mulholland Clothiers' depiction of a giant cardinal standing in triumphant pose over a fallen cougar. Other shop windows held large posters urging the Cardinals to victory.

For Joe and the other players, there was little opportunity to admire all the handiwork aimed at the game. Their grueling practice sessions ended as darkness fell. They walked home, weary and ready for dinner, and then turned from football to homework.

Joe's parents seemed to be striving to keep the swelling excitement from entering their home. Joe had seen it before, in advance of an important game. His father always greeted him with the usual, "How was practice?" And Joe replied, as always, "Fine." His mother said, "We're ready to eat, wash up." And Joe gave his usual reply, almost automatically, "I just had a shower." It was becoming a family joke. And, through it all, nobody in the Mitchell household mentioned the banners and posters all over town, or even Hoytville High by name.

Joe had decided on Monday to do as Coach Holliman asked and not even mention to his family the new plays. Joe could imagine his father's mouth falling open when he caught a pass from Tracy.

Finally, Friday arrived.

The practice sessions were behind them. All that remained now was the game. The season was behind them, except for this one game.

And, Joe reflected, somewhat to his own surprise, his football career at Hillcrest High was behind him, except for this one game. It was almost over.

Letting Mrs. Armitage's calculus instruction drone on unheard, Joe tilted his head slightly and stared out the window.

Probably, he concluded, he never would run through a practice session again with Coley and Tracy and Lew in the backfield with him.

The thought troubled him less than he could have imagined a week earlier.

Mrs. Armitage's voice cut through his thoughts. "Joe, the game is tonight. This morning, it's calculus."

Joe gave a little smile and nod and then focused on the figures Mrs. Armitage had scrawled on the board. "Yes, okay," he said.

He moved through the rest of his classes with the minutes dragging by. He felt none of the nervousness that had hit him before the Marianna game. But he was eager to get on with the game.

Then it was time for the pep rally—his last one at Hillcrest High, he realized.

As he walked into the auditorium with Tracy, heading for the steps leading up to the stage, he wondered why it was only now dawning on him that this was the last time. His first pep rally, two years and a couple of months ago, when he was a tenth grader, seemed now like only yesterday. He remembered that he had been nervous on that day, standing on the stage with the older players, the juniors and seniors. But that night he was the starting quarterback and passed for three touchdowns, and he never was nervous again about standing on the stage with the older players.

Joe saw Coley and Lew, already on the stage with some of the other players, and he turned and looked at Tracy, and then back at his two friends ahead of him on the stage. None of them seemed to be thinking this was the last time. Coley was excited, his eyes aglow, as always. Lew was deadpan, as always. Tracy was grinning and waving to someone, as if this was just another day.

Joe and Tracy climbed the steps to the stage and walked across to join the others.

The cheerleaders were in a line at the front of the stage, leading a roaring cheer.

Off to the side, Coach Holliman approached the lectern. He stood a moment, frowning at the audience, until the cheerleaders finished and ran to the side of the stage. Then, as the noise died down, he leaned into the microphone.

"This is the last game—"

A lot of shouting erupted, and he stepped back until it subsided.

"This is the last game of the season," he began again, "and the last game at Hillcrest High for our seniors. They will graduate and then move on in different directions with their lives. This is the last game our seniors will play together."

Joe kept his eyes on Coach Holliman.

# Chapter 16

◆　　　　　　　Joe and the other seniors on the team, nine of them in all, walked in a line toward the center of the field to meet the Hoytville cocaptains for the coin toss. This being their last game for Hillcrest High, each senior was designated a cocaptain by Coach Holliman.

The bleachers on both sides of the field were filled to overflowing. People were seated in the aisles and on the steps. Behind the end zones special rows of folding chairs were set up to try to accommodate the crowd. But even there, people were standing behind them.

It seemed that all of Hillcrest was at the game, and also probably half of Hoytville had arrived in a caravan of cars following the team bus.

Even as the players approached the referee for the coin toss, the noise of the fans and the two competing pep bands was deafening.

At the center of the field there was a lot of

handshaking with the two Hoytville cocaptains, and some mumbling of names. Then the referee spun the coin into the air and let it fall to the ground.

One of the Hoytville cocaptains said, "Heads."

The referee bent, peered at the coin, and said, "Tails. Hillcrest High wins the toss." He turned to Joe. "Will you kick or receive?"

"Receive," Joe said.

The referee turned to the Hoytville cocaptains and asked which end of the field they wanted to defend. On this clear, windless night, it made little difference. A Hoytville cocaptain chose the end to Joe's right.

Then the referee went through his motions, signaling the outcome of the coin toss and the decisions that had been made.

Joe and the other seniors turned and ran back to the sideline and into the leaping, shouting crowd of Hillcrest High Cardinals.

On both sides of the field and in the areas behind the end zones, too, everyone was standing—and, for sure, everyone was shouting. The noise of the shouting, punctuated by the thumping sounds of the pep bands, seemed to vibrate in the glare of the arc lights.

Then the kickoff teams took up their positions on the field, with Coley dropping back to the twelve-yard line to await the kick.

* * *

The Hoytville kicker backed Coley to the ten-yard line with a high boomer down the middle of the field. Coley took in the ball and raced to his right, toward the sideline in front of the Cardinals' bench. His teammates were picking off the charging Hoytville tacklers and backing into position to form a wall for Coley's run along the sideline.

Coley crossed the twenty-yard line, then the twenty-five, but he never made it to the forming wall of blockers. A Hoytville tackler, seeming to sense from the beginning what was happening, had veered sharply and, bumping past a Hill-crest blocker, slammed Coley to the ground at the twenty-six-yard line.

Joe, stepping forward at the sideline to watch the play, felt his heart leap into his throat when he saw Coley, legs still churning, leave the ground in the grasp of the tackler and then crash to earth beneath him.

For one horrible second Coley didn't get up. Then he leaped to his feet and jogged to the sideline for his moment of rest during the first play from scrimmage.

Joe pulled on his helmet and headed onto the field. Passing Coley, he said, "Okay?"

Coley nodded.

Lining up behind Charlie Garrison for the first play, Joe nodded subconsciously as he scanned the Hoytville defensive alignment. There was no doubt somebody had seen the opening-play pass against Marianna the week before and duly reported on it to the Cougars. The linemen were bunched tight, ready for the charge, but the linebackers were not up close, and not that extra step in toward the middle of the line that would signify they were sure a line plunge was coming. Maybe there was going to be a plunge. But then again, maybe not.

Joe handed off to Lew and sent him plunging into the left side of the line, the standard Hillcrest High game-opening play. So much for passing on the first play. Lew battled his way forward for three yards before going down in a heap of Hoytville tacklers.

Joe, dancing back away from the collision after handing off the ball, could not escape a scary thought. If that was the weaker side of the Hoytville line, what was going to happen when he tried to send a ball carrier plunging into the right side of the line? But he noticed that, yes, the left linebacker did leap forward quickly—a little too quickly—in an effort to shore up his side of the line. There was going to be room to pass behind him.

Tracy gained four yards on a wide sweep around right end and Joe sliced off left tackle on a keeper for four yards and a first down on the thirty-seven-yard line.

The Cardinals were moving in their first possession, and the noise from the crowd all around the field increased several decibels.

Joe leaned into the huddle and called for a pass to Tracy cutting behind the left-side linebacker, who always was too quick to leap forward to help stop a line plunge.

Lining up, Joe looked at the linebackers. The one on the right was supposed to telegraph a blitz by standing with one foot forward. But he did not have one foot forward. Okay, no blitz. Maybe.

Joe took the snap, turned, and extended the ball to Lew, who was throwing himself into the left side of the line. At the last moment Joe pulled the ball back, sending Lew into the line empty-handed. Holding the ball low, Joe rolled back. The left-side linebacker was lunging forward, going for Lew. Beyond him, Tracy was loping into empty space. The defensive back was moving up, toward Tracy.

Joe brought up the ball, cocked, and fired.

Just as he sent the ball on its way, he heard the shouted word—"Pass!"—from somewhere in the tangle of bodies at the line of scrimmage.

The linebacker, already committed to helping his forward wall stop Lew, slammed on the brakes, stood up, and threw a hand wildly in the air.

He was a very lucky linebacker. His thrusting

hand nicked the rifling ball above his head.

The ball went up, floating gently, an invitation to an interception. The linebacker whirled, looking for the ball in the air. Tracy cut sharply and dashed toward it, arms outstretched, with the defensive back now right behind him.

The ball was falling. The linebacker spotted the ball and, off-balance, tried a lunge that failed. Tracy made a dive that came up short. The ball hit the ground.

Joe resumed breathing.

Then, as if the deflected pass signaled the end of good things, Coley got caught for a three-yard loss and Joe, dodging a tackler, overthrew Tracy running a crossing pattern designed to gain fifteen yards and the needed first down in one play.

Harry Pearson trotted onto the field to punt, and Joe, pulling off his helmet, jogged to the sideline.

Joe glanced at Coach Holliman to see if the coach had anything to say to him. But the coach was already moving down the sideline, his intense stare turned to the field where the Cardinals were going to put their defense up against the Hoytville Cougars for the first time.

Joe turned to the field and watched Harry's punt—a good enough kick, but the Hoytville runner returned it to the Hoytville thirty-eight-yard line.

"Sorry," said Coley, coming up alongside Joe.

Joe turned to him. Coley was referring to the three-yard loss on second down. An arm tackle had brought the tiny running back down. A stronger player might have bulled his way through the tackle and gained yardage. "Next time," Joe said. "Next time we'll get 'em."

"Yeah."

They stood together, watching the Hoytville Cougars grind forward with a series of short gains, the runners pounding into the line. Three yards, five yards, four yards—a first down on the midfield stripe. Then three, three, and four for a first down on the Hillcrest forty-yard line.

Joe glanced at the scoreboard clock to his right. The first quarter was more than half gone. By this time, he thought, the Cardinals should have positioned themselves for one of the new plays. Coach Holliman wanted to run them early in the game. That way, even if the plays failed to click for huge gains, they would give the Hoytville defense something new and unexpected to worry about. The known threat of a double reverse would force the Hoytville defense into caution on all end sweeps. Once Tracy threw a pass, he became a double threat any time he handled the ball.

But the clock was ticking and the Hoytville Cougars looked unstoppable.

Then the Hillcrest defense stiffened. The middle of the line held the plunging fullback to a gain of only one yard. On the next play, Art Baldwin, the Cardinals' left linebacker and the leader of the defense, stopped a runner going off tackle for a three-yard gain.

Third down and six for the Cougars.

The Hoytville quarterback, walking to his huddle, gave it all away when he glanced at his coach at the sideline and nodded at the signal he received. He was asking about a pass, and he got an affirmative answer. Joe had gotten caught in exactly the same mistake once as a tenth grader, and Coach Holliman had pointed out the error in no uncertain terms.

Joe almost grinned when the Cougars lined up for the snap.

When the Hoytville quarterback took the snap, Joe cupped his hands at his mouth and shouted, "Pass!"

Art either heard Joe's shout or spotted something telltale in the way the Hoytville quarterback moved. Art held his ground instead of charging forward to meet yet another line plunge. Then he picked up the receiver coming out of the backfield.

The quarterback, with his primary receiver covered by Art, frantically looked around the field for another choice. His big forward wall was giving him time for the search. He found nothing attractive and looked back at the player being tracked by Art.

The receiver made a quick cut and went wide, getting himself open for a moment, and the quarterback fired the ball.

Art came across in front of the receiver and grabbed the ball. The big linebacker stood flat-footed and still for a fraction of a second at the thirty-yard line, clutching the ball in both hands. Then he began running, and churned eleven yards to the Hillcrest forty-one-yard line before a couple of Hoytville tacklers brought him down.

Joe pulled on his helmet and raced onto the field.

The Cardinals were on what Coach Holliman called "the good side of the forty"—in territory where they could risk one of the new plays. The coach wanted no chances taken with the likes of a double reverse or halfback pass deep in the Cardinals' own territory. In their game plan, the forty-yard line was the magic stripe.

Joe grinned at Tracy in the huddle. "Okay, ol' rifle-arm, this is your moment."

Tracy did not grin back. He nodded somberly.

Joe took the snap, turned, and ran a few yards to his left behind the line. Then he stopped, turned back, and flipped the ball to Tracy, running to the right. Tracy took in the short pass and continued to the right. Joe drifted on, drawing no one's attention. The Hoytville defenders were going the other way, toward Tracy. When Tracy cut, and then stopped, Joe broke into a full-speed run straight ahead.

Even the Hoytville defensive back on Joe's side of the field had taken the bait, edging forward and now toward Tracy's side of the field.

Joe flew past him and looked back. He heard, as if in the distance, the shouts of "Pass!" Out of the corner of his eye, he saw the defensive back shift gears and start toward him. The ball was there, up in the air. It looked big. But it seemed to hang there, as if not moving. Was this the way his passes looked to his receivers?

The ball was coming down short. Joe slowed his pace to put himself under it. Finally, the ball arrived. Joe caught it and tucked it away.

The defensive back, helped by Joe's need to slow for the ball falling short, was bearing down on him. Joe veered slightly in an effort to gain a step. The defensive back got a hand on Joe, then another. Joe whirled furiously.

The hands slipped away and Joe ran to the goal.

# Chapter 17

◆      The scoreboard blinked: Cardinals 6, Visitors 0—as Joe jogged out of the end zone into a mob of teammates.

A beaming Tracy was shouting—"Man-oh-man!"—and a laughing Joe called out to him, "Ol' rifle-arm."

Through the crowd of cheering players around him, Joe spotted Coach Holliman at the sideline. His scowl seemed even deeper than his usual gametime frown. Probably scoring on a trick play did not go down well with the conservative coach. To him, football games were won with running and blocking, tackling and passing—not with trickery. But Joe had no such qualms. To him, all that mattered was that the play had worked, the Cardinals had scored. Joe gave a broad smile to Coach Holliman's frown.

Then the teams lined up for the try for the extra point. Joe took his position and knelt to take the snap and hold for Harry Pearson's kick.

Charlie Garrison snapped the ball from center. Joe caught it and placed it down. Harry stepped forward and kicked. The ball tumbled end over end through the uprights. The score was 7–0.

But the elation was short-lived for the cheering Hillcrest High players and their roaring fans all around the field. The Hoytville Cougars took Harry's kickoff and then, sticking to their ground game, methodically plowed their way down the field. They hit the left side of the line, then the right, then the center. They did not make the mistake of tipping their hand on a pass play. They did not pass at all. The only variation to the pounding plunges into the line was an occasional end run. Never anything fancy, just a strong runner carrying the ball behind strong blockers.

As the powerful machine moved down the field, the noise from the Hillcrest High fans faded and was replaced by the cheers from the Hoytville fans seated together in the bleacher across the field from the Cardinals' bench.

The Cougars scored on the thirteenth play of the drive, the last play of the first quarter, and their kicker tied the score at 7–7.

The Cougars' kickoff was high and short, forcing Coley to run forward to the eighteen-yard line to make the catch. The high, floating

kick, coming down short, had given the Hoytville tacklers time to charge down the field
and arrive just as Coley was taking in the ball.
Coley found himself instantly surrounded,
seemingly trapped. But he wriggled his way
through a forest of outstretched hands, manag-
ing to reach the twenty-four-yard line before going down.

Hoping the memory of the halfback pass was
still fresh in the minds of the Hoytville defenders, Joe pitched out to Tracy racing around right
end, and moved himself to the left, pretending
to position himself for a race downfield as a pass
receiver. Nobody seemed to be fooled, but Tracy
gained five yards. Then Coley picked up four on
a pitchout to the left and Lew, hitting the left
side of the line, got the needed one yard for a
first down on the thirty-four-yard line.

Joe ran a keeper off right tackle, fighting for
two yards behind Skip Matthews, to set up the
next play—a pass to Tracy behind the left linebacker.

This time, the linebacker who liked to jump
forward too quickly was not lucky. When Joe
faked a handoff to Lew plunging into the left
side of the line, the linebacker leaped. And when
Joe withdrew the ball and rolled back and to his
left and threw to Tracy, nobody gave the shouted
warning, "Pass!" Joe's pass zipped into Tracy's
hands at the forty-four-yard line. The alert de-

fensive back nailed him immediately, but the play gained another first down.

And the Cardinals were again on the "good side of the forty."

Walking to the huddle, Joe turned to the sideline and gave Coach Holliman a questioning glance. The coach knew Joe's question, with the Cardinals having crossed the forty-yard line. He nodded slightly and held up both forefingers. Yes, go ahead with the double reverse.

In the huddle, Joe called the play. Then he paused a second and looked at the linemen— Skip Matthews, Charlie Garrison, the others. "You guys have got to hold them," he said. "This is going to take a little time, you know."

The linemen nodded and Joe broke the huddle.

Moving into his stance behind the center, Joe looked at the massive Hoytville linemen and recalled Coach Holliman's statement: "Even if it doesn't work for a large gain, the fact that we've got the play will add to the pressure on the Cougars on every end run."

Joe took the snap, turned, and extended the ball to Tracy running to the right. Tracy took in the ball on the dead run. Four steps later, with the Hoytville defense shifting to meet him, Tracy extended the ball in his right hand to Coley running left. Coley clutched the ball with both hands.

Somebody in the Hoytville defense shouted, "Reverse!"

The defenders were shifting back to meet the changed flow of the ball.

Joe stepped forward and reached out to take the ball from Coley for yet another reversal of the flow.

He saw the blur of a Hoytville tackler out of the corner of his eye. Then he felt a jarring bump as the tackler tried to fight his way past Joe to get at Coley. Joe threw himself into the tackler, a block to set Coley free.

But Coley already had the ball out for Joe.

Somebody, maybe the falling tackler or maybe even Joe, bumped the ball as Coley was trying to bring it back in. The ball shot out of his hand, back toward the goal. It hit the ground and took one bounce, again toward the goal, before a white-jerseyed Hoytville defender covered it on the twenty-five-yard line.

Joe leaped to his feet, consciously avoiding a glance at the number of the Hoytville player who had broken through and turned the play into a disaster. Joe did not want to know which of the Hillcrest High linemen had failed to hold his man. Without a word to anyone, he turned and headed for the sideline through the Hillcrest High defensive players coming onto the field.

The Hoytville Cougars scored in seven plays and kicked good, taking a 14–7 lead.

* * *

First the Cardinals and then the Cougars sputtered on offense and had to punt the ball away, as the clock ticked past the midway point of the second quarter.

"First play after Coley's back in the game," Coach Holliman said to Joe, "run the double reverse but tell Tracy to keep the ball and keep going wide to the right."

Joe and the coach were standing at the sideline, Joe pulling on his helmet. On the field the referee was placing the ball on the Hillcrest High thirty-nine-yard line, where Coley had gone down returning Hoytville's first punt of the game. The Hillcrest High defense, realigned with a third linebacker, had held the Cougars, forcing the punt.

Joe nodded acknowledgment of Coach Holliman's instruction as he turned and ran onto the field, passing Coley heading for the sideline and his one play of rest following the punt return.

Joe sent Lew thundering off right tackle. Lew battled his way through the strong side of the Hoytville line for three yards.

Coley came racing back into the game, and Joe called the play, sending Tracy sweeping around right end while he and Coley played their roles in the double reverse.

When Joe spun and extended the ball to Tracy running by, he heard the thumps and thuds of the battle in the line behind him. When Tracy took the ball in full stride and raced for the sideline, Joe moved on a couple of steps, as he had in the reverse. Coley ran by Tracy, but did not take the ball. Joe turned and looked at the Hoytville defense.

As expected, the Cougars were hesitating before turning to pursue Tracy. They were waiting to see if he handed off to another player running in the opposite direction. The hesitation lasted one second, maybe two. But it was enough.

Tracy turned the corner outside the end, got a needed block, and ran twenty-one yards to the Hoytville thirty-seven-yard line before a defensive back slammed into him and knocked him out of bounds.

From there, Lew got four yards, and then three, hitting the left side of the line. Joe, on a keeper off left tackle, bulled his way five yards to a first down on the Hoytville twenty-five-yard line.

Then Joe passed to Benjy Moore at the sideline for six yards and to Coley in the left flat for seven, placing the Cardinals on the Hoytville twelve-yard line with a first down.

While the officials moved the chains, Joe looked at Coach Holliman. The question was whether to run, and hope for a succession of short gains through the huge forward wall, or pass. Lew was marking up short gains in the line. But he was being stopped on occasion, too. The yardage was going to come harder here in the shadow of the goal. The passing had gone well—to Tracy, Coley, and Benjy. It was the coach's decision to make.

Coach Holliman brought his right hand up to his ear—pass.

Joe threw over center to Tracy in the end zone, and a backpedaling linebacker batted the ball away. Then he sent Tracy into the left corner of the end zone and Coley into the right corner, and threw over center to Benjy. But a linebacker had picked up the tight end coming across and arrived in time to knock the ball away.

It was third down and ten yards to go.

With the linebackers playing a step deep, expecting a pass, Joe threw to Tracy crossing behind the line of scrimmage. Tracy caught the ball in front of a linebacker, angled toward the goal—and ran into the arms of the linebacker. He went down on the six-yard line.

Fourth down and four.

Walking to the huddle, Joe turned toward Coach Holliman on the sideline. Coach Holliman held up two fingers: a Lew Preston plunge.

Joe frowned. He wanted to throw to Tracy in the end zone. But, yes, maybe that was what the Hoytville defenders were expecting. Clearly, the Cardinals preferred passing to running against the huge line. Maybe a plunge would catch them off guard. He nodded his understanding to the coach.

Joe took the snap and handed off the ball to Lew, hitting the left side of the line. Then Joe quickly straightened and cocked his right arm, hoping to freeze, if only for a second, the quick-jumping linebacker. But it didn't work. Hoytville's left side of the line, with the linebacker's help, stopped Lew for no gain.

A whooping cheer of triumph went up from the crowd of Hoytville fans.

Joe lowered his head and walked off the field.

For the remainder of the second quarter, the two teams took turns driving to midfield, then bogging down in the face of determined defensive play, and finally having to punt.

The first half ended with the scoreboard showing: Cardinals 7, Visitors 14.

In the dressing room, Joe was seated on a bench, leaning back against a locker, breathing deeply and staring at nothing, when he heard Coley's voice from ten feet away.

"I have something to say," Coley announced to the room at large. His voice was louder than the usual conversational tone, but far short of a shout. He was speaking loudly enough to be heard throughout the quiet dressing room, but no more.

Joe looked at his friend with surprise and brought himself forward, leaning with his elbows on his knees.

Coley was looking directly at Joe.

All around the room, players turned in Coley's direction.

Joe glanced around the room for Coach Holliman. The coach seldom made dressing room speeches himself, and never allowed anyone else to do it. Joe remembered the time, the previous season, when Tracy decided to exhort the Cardinals to greater effort. Coach Holliman had cut him off with a curt: "If there are going to be any speeches, I'll be the one to make them." Now what was the coach going to say?

Joe found Coach Holliman turning from a player at the far side of the room. He was frowning, of course. But he also, to Joe's surprise, had a questioning look on his face. He was going to let Coley speak. The coach thrust his hands in his trouser pockets and waited, along with everyone else in the room.

Coley looked at Coach Holliman, too. Probably he remembered what happened when Tracy tried to address the team. Coley paused a moment, as if giving the coach a chance to stop him, and then looked back at Joe.

For a moment, Coley looked like he regretted having taken command of the dressing room.

Then he clenched his jaw and glanced around at his teammates, ending with his gaze again on Joe, and began speaking.

"For some of us—the seniors—this is the last game. Some of us may play football in college, but we'll be at different colleges. Some of us won't play football in college. Some of us may not even go to college. So this is our last game."

Coley was still looking at Joe, as if speaking only to him.

Joe frowned as he watched. Coley has figured it out, he thought. There is no more backfield package after tonight. Joe would be going to Randolph, or someplace else. The others in the backfield would be going to Ryder State, or someplace else. The four of them won't be together.

Joe glanced at Tracy, then Lew. They were watching Coley. Joe turned back to Coley. When had Coley figured it out? Joe couldn't guess. He didn't know when he had decided himself. There was that moment in the corridor with Coach Holliman on Saturday, but that was just the first time he had faced the fact. Surely, he had made his decision before that and just couldn't face it. Maybe, he thought, Coley figured it out before I did.

"Our last game together, that's what this is," Coley said.

When Coley stopped and swallowed hard, Joe

thought for a horrifying moment that his friend was going to break into tears. Coley was always emotional. He got more excited before a game than anyone else on the team. He exulted in victory and suffered through losses more than anyone.

But Coley, without tears, took a breath and continued. "After all the good games, I don't want to have to spend the rest of my life remembering that the last game—our last game together—was a loss." He paused. "And you don't, either."

After another moment of silence, he said, "That's all."

Coach Holliman immediately said, "Let's go. It's time."

The coach's voice startled Joe, and apparently everyone else, too. All eyes turned to the coach, and then the players began getting to their feet and filing silently out the door.

## Chapter 18

Returning to the field for the start of the second half, Joe broke into a jog. Eyes down, he looked neither left nor right. He was aware of other players jogging along with him. But he did not want to know whose faces belonged to those blurs moving around him.

If his eyes met Tracy's, his friend was certain to ask, "What was that all about?" Joe did not want to try to answer. Not now, for sure.

If Lew were the player at Joe's side, he would say nothing. But his expression would ask for an explanation. Joe did not want to try to explain just yet.

Least of all did he want to see Coley next to him.

They had a game to finish. There would be time later to talk of other things. They could talk all night, if they wanted to. But now they had to keep their minds on the game. Yes, Joe told himself, keep your own mind on the game.

A huge cheer erupted as Joe led the jogging crowd of players through the gate in the chain-link fence and onto the field, heading for the bench.

Joe broke into a full-speed run to the bench and the others followed.

The cheers rolling down from the bleachers grew louder as the players ganged together in front of the bench, shouting and slapping one another on the shoulder pads.

Joe looked at the packed bleachers and then at the field, empty and waiting, and thought that the last half of the last game was beginning.

The clock showed five and a half minutes remaining in the game. The scoreboard lights showed: Cardinals 15, Visitors 21.

The two teams had battled through the third quarter and most of the fourth quarter on even terms, each scoring one touchdown—tempting evidence to each side that there might be more to come. It was evidence to the Cardinals that they might score again and win the game. For Hoytville, it was evidence that the Cougars might score once more and seal the victory.

The Cougars had taken Harry Pearson's second-half kickoff and marched down the field—sixty-seven yards in twelve plays—to increase their lead to 21–7. The Cougars had seemed unstoppable in their drive to the end zone. But after that, the Cardinals' defense, led by Art Baldwin, stopped them every time.

The Cardinals had narrowed the gap on the first play of the fourth quarter when Joe shot through right tackle behind Skip Matthews's block, broke two tackles, and ran thirty-one yards to the goal. Then, aiming for victory instead of a tie, the Cardinals went for a two-point conversion. Joe got it, running wide to the left behind Lew and Tracy.

But now the clock was a formidable foe of the Hillcrest High Cardinals. Time was running out.

On the field, the Cardinals' defense had stalled the Cougars one more time. The punting teams were going onto the field, with the ball at the Hillcrest High forty-one-yard line.

Joe glanced at the clock and then down the field at Coley, standing at the ten-yard line, arms hanging loose, waiting. Joe thought that if his friend was ever going to break away for a long return, this was the time.

But the Hoytville punter did not give Coley a kick to return. He aimed his punt toward the corner, trying to send the ball out of bounds near the goal, leaving the Cardinals with their backs to their own goal and five minutes remaining.

He missed the corner. The ball bounced into the end zone for a touchback.

Joe pulled on his helmet and ran onto the field to take up the attack at the twenty-yard line.

Eighty yards to go. Five minutes to do it.

Joe passed to Tracy at the left sideline for seven yards and hit Coley at the right sideline for six and a first down on the thirty-three-yard line.

Then he sent Tracy running to the right. Tracy gained four yards and, just as important, ran out of bounds, stopping the clock at a little more than four minutes to go.

On the next play Joe sent Tracy running right again. But this time Tracy ran four steps, stopped, turned, and threw back to the left where Joe was drifting into the flat—the halfback pass play that got the Cardinals their first touchdown.

Joe was all alone.

But the pass, a wobbler, was short and hit the ground in front of the diving Joe's outstretched hands.

Joe passed to Benjy at the sideline for four yards. The tight end unwisely tried for more yardage after the catch instead of stepping out of bounds and stopping the clock.

Third down and two to go on the forty-one-yard line with the clock still running.

Joe saw Coach Holliman making a *T* with his hands, and called a time-out, stopping the clock. It was the Cardinals' last time-out, but they needed desperately to stop the clock, and clearly this was a time for the coach and the quarterback to talk. Joe jogged to the sideline where Coach Holliman waited.

"You can get two yards and the first down behind Skip," the coach said.

Joe nodded and waited.

"Then try Coley on a pitchout. It's the pass that they're afraid of. They're beginning to set themselves for a pass on every down. Maybe we can catch them off balance, and maybe Coley can get into the open."

Joe nodded again. Yes, the prospect of Coley running loose in a broken field spelled yardage, if not touchdown.

"Then hit the middle—Lew—once," Coach Holliman continued. "After Coley's run, they'll be doubly certain a pass is coming. If Lew can break through, he ought to find some running room in the secondary."

Joe automatically turned and looked at the clock. Three minutes and seven seconds remaining. His plunge for the first down would take time. Coley's run would take time. Could they afford another running play eating up time?

"Plenty of time," Coach Holliman said. "Then you throw into the end zone."

"Okay." Joe nodded, returned to the huddle, and called the play.

Taking the snap, he rolled out to his right, ducked his shoulder in a fake into the line, and shoveled the ball out wide to Coley.

Coley took in the pitch just short of the line of scrimmage at the forty-one. The linemen and the linebacker had followed Joe's fake. Now they were recovering. But Coley had running room.

As Coley ran across the forty-five-yard line, eluding the reach of a defensive end, the fans in the bleachers leapt to their feet with a roar.

Coley, twisting, turning, changing direction half a dozen times, gained the nineteen-yard line before one defensive back slowed him and another tackled him.

Joe, rushing down the field to the huddle, glanced at the clock—barely two minutes remaining.

He looked to his left, toward Coach Holliman at the sideline. The coach, his hands out, palms down in a calming gesture, nodded his head once.

Joe gave the ball to Lew straight up the middle. As Coach Holliman had predicted, the defense was braced for a pass, with the linebackers blitzing. Lew broke through the line, found open space, and gained nine yards to the ten. But his run ate up valuable seconds.

The clock showed a minute and a half remaining, and was still ticking. The Cardinals had no more time-outs.

Joe knew what to do next. He called a quarterback sneak. A one-yard gain would win a first down and stop the clock for the movement of the chain.

Joe took the snap, clutched the ball to his stomach with both hands, and pushed forward, twisting a few precious inches around a tackler before he went down.

He had the first down—or did he?

The referee ordered the chain brought onto the field for a-measurement. Joe bent into the crowd and watched as the referee placed the chain on the ground.

By three or four inches—a finger's length—the tip of the ball was beyond the chain.

Joe let out a cheer, and the referee swung his arm in the signal of a first down.

In the huddle, Joe looked at the faces turned toward him. This close to the goal, there was not going to be any room for open-field running by Coley. Lew was not going to find the middle open to him this time. Tracy, slow afoot, was not going to score around end. It was up to Joe—passing, or running if his receivers weren't open. It was Joe who had to get the Cardinals across the goal.

Joe overthrew Tracy in the left side of the end zone. He had to, with the defensive halfback shadowing Tracy step for step. A faster receiver would have pulled away and made the catch.

He threw again to Tracy in the end zone. The defensive back slapped the ball down, and came heart-stoppingly close to picking off the pass.

Joe sent Coley into the end zone and, while the shifty little running back ducked and dodged trying to get free, a Hoytville tackler broke through. Joe tucked the ball away and ran to the right, aiming for the sideline to stop the clock if he failed to reach the end zone.

He reached neither. Two tacklers brought him down on the five-yard line, inbounds.

Joe leaped to his feet, turning to look at the clock.

Less than thirty seconds remained.

Joe shouted: "Hurry! Hurry! No huddle! No huddle!"

He stepped up behind Charlie Garrison and called out, "Wide left!" He was telling his team-mates which way the ball was going to go, either a pass to Tracy or a run by Joe. He was also telling the astonished Hoytville defenders. But Joe knew that Tracy would be out there, ready for a pass, and that he would have blockers going left. "On two," he called out.

"One . . . "

The buzzer sounded.

Joe straightened up, stunned.

The game was over. The Cardinals had lost.

In front of him, on both sides of the goal line—so near, yet never to be crossed again on this night—the Hoytville players erupted in a celebration of victory. They shouted and cheered, hugging and clapping one another on the shoulder pads.

From a single section of the bleachers on the far side, a cheer went up from the Hoytville fans, and the Hoytville pep band swung into an anthem of triumph.

In the end zones and the other sections of the bleachers, there was total silence.

The Hoytville players began running and leaping and skipping toward their sideline, where the other members of the squad were pouring onto the field to meet them.

Joe turned and saw Coley, tears streaming down his face. Joe put his arm around Coley's shoulder and they walked off the field with the other Cardinals.

Joe and Coley were seated next to each other on a bench in the deathly silent Hillcrest High dressing room. Tracy and Lew were seated on a bench across from them. None had made the first move toward undressing for the showers.

Joe wondered why he didn't feel like banging his locker with his helmet in anger and frustration. But all he felt was weariness and a sense of regret. He was sorry he had not been able to pull it out for the rest of them. Then he spoke the one word. "Sorry."

Before any of the others could speak, Coach Holliman's frowning face appeared in their midst. He leaned in toward Joe. "You were great," he said. "You were as great in those last five minutes as I've ever seen." He kept his eyes on Joe for a long moment, then looked around at the others. He said, "They beat us, but I am very proud of every one of you."

Joe nodded.

Coley screwed up his face, and for a moment seemed about to break into tears again. Then he got himself under control.

Tracy said, "But we lost."

Coach Holliman almost smiled. Then he said, "Sometimes that happens." He gave a little nod and walked away.

Joe stared at the back of the departing coach. The coach had wanted the victory and the championship as much as any of them, maybe more. Joe repeated the single word of apology to the coach's back, "Sorry." Unhearing, Coach Holliman was approaching the sweat-streaked and somber Art Baldwin, the senior linebacker who time and again had come up with the big play needed to stop the Cougars.

Coley took a deep breath and said, "So the backfield package comes to an end with a loss."

Joe stared straight ahead, at a spot on Lew's shoulder pad, and said nothing.

Nobody spoke for a moment. Then Tracy said,

"What do you mean—comes to an end?"

Joe glanced at Tracy. His friend's face wore the questioning expression of a person beginning to realize that something is going on but is unable to identify it. Tracy, so wrapped up in his problems with his father on the question of Ryder State, had failed to notice any of the clues that indicated Joe was drawing away. Tracy had listened to Coley's suspicions but, typically Tracy, he had let them float by while concentrating on his own concerns.

Joe looked from Tracy to Lew. His friend did not seem puzzled. Lew, who seldom had much to say, seemed to know what Coley was talking about.

"Joe's not going to Ryder State," Coley said. "Joe's going to Randolph or some other bigtime football school." He looked up at Tracy. "And you're probably not going to Ryder State, either, you know." He gave a little grin. "Maybe Lew and I will go to Ryder State together."

Tracy went wide-eyed. "What is all this all of a sudden? Have I missed something?" He was looking from one to the other, and his eyes finally came to rest on Joe. "Is this true?"

Joe looked across at Tracy. "I think so. Maybe. Probably."

"But I thought—"

Joe would not have picked the dressing room in the moments after a loss to Hoytville as the place and time to discuss his future plans with his friends. But, he thought with a small shrug, at least the subject had been kept under wraps until after the last game had been played.

"I've decided that I've got to look into all of the possibilities," he said to Tracy. Then he added, "Sort of like your father has been saying to you."

Tracy frowned across at him. "So that's what Coley's speech was all about, huh?" he said. "I thought so."

"You did?"

"Sure. That's what my father has been saying all along, especially after that story out of Randolph and then the article in the St. Louis paper. He said that you were never going to some little state college in Indiana to play football."

Joe nodded slightly and said only, "Uh-huh, I remember."

"And you didn't really deny it," Tracy said.

Joe looked across at Tracy and said, "I know, but I just wasn't sure myself then."

Joe turned to Coley at his side. "And you? When did you know?"

"I've thought you were moving in that direction for a long time, but I didn't want to press it. I was hoping I was wrong, even when that business with Tracy's father came up. But then, well, just watching you play in the first half out there tonight, well, it looked like you belonged at Randolph or someplace like that." He paused.

"And I knew this was our last game together."

Joe managed a smile at his friend. "I didn't think I looked so good in the first half," he said.

"You did," Coley said, "and that's why I decided to say what I did at the halftime."

Joe looked at Lew. "And you knew," he said.

Lew nodded. "I knew last year—knew that you were good enough to go places, places the rest of us couldn't go."

Joe wrinkled his brow. "Really? You really thought that last year?"

Lew nodded matter-of-factly and said simply, "Sure."

Joe looked from Lew to Tracy to Coley. "I'll tell you something," he said finally. "No matter where we go, we'll always be the backfield package."

After a moment, Joe stood. "We'd better shower and dress or we'll be late for the party in the gym." He began pulling his jersey off over his head.

"We'll go to the house later," Tracy said, bending to untie a shoelace.

"Yeah," Joe said.